RUN FOR
YOUR LIFE

ALSO BY SILVANA GANDOLFI

BOOKS IN ENGLISH

Aldabra, or the Tortoise Who Loved Shakespeare

BOOKS IN ITALIAN

La scimmia nella biglia
Pasta di drago
Occhio al gatto
L'isola del tempo perso
La memoria dell'acqua
Aldabra
Qui vicino mio Ariel
La bambina in fondo al mare
Io dentro gli spari
Il club degli amici immaginari

RUN FOR YOUR LIFE

Silvana Gandolfi

Translated from the Italian by
LYNNE SHARON SCHWARTZ

Restless Books
for Young Readers

This book has been published with a translation grant awarded by the Italian
Ministry of Foreign Affairs and International Cooperation.

First Restless Books paperback edition June 2018

Paperback ISBN: 9781632061652
Library of Congress Control Number: 2017944637

Cover design by Aimee Fleck
Set in Garibaldi by Tetragon, London

Printed in Canada

10 9 8 7 6 5 4 3 2 1

Restless Books, Inc.
232 3rd Street, Suite A111
Brooklyn, NY 11215

www.restlessbooks.org
publisher@restlessbooks.org

To Fede, he knows why

AUTHOR'S NOTE

Sicily is a fertile and beautiful island located opposite the southern tip of Italy (known as the "toe of the boot" because of its shape) and separated from the mainland by the Strait of Messina. In ancient times, it was strongly influenced by classical Greek culture, and during later centuries it was invaded by a variety of colonizers, both Western and Islamic. All of them have left traces on Sicily's landscape and culture, making it a fascinating island, full of contradictions. It became part of Italy in 1860.

In the nineteenth century, most Sicilians were poor peasants who worked the lands belonging to a few wealthy proprietors. That period saw the origin of the Mafia, a group that claimed to protect both peasants and landowners. It soon split into rival clans and degenerated into an organized crime syndicate, using threats, violence, and murder to retain power. Today the Mafia is the worst enemy of that spectacular island.

This novel, although inspired by actual events, is a work of imagination. I took the liberty of creating things that don't exist, such as the town of Tonduzzo, 33A Vicolo dello Zingaro, and many other specific details. Certain things, however, are real: the Livorno–Palermo ferry, the monument in front of the Palace of Justice, the names carved on the stairs, the newsstand in Piazza della Kalsa.

And in Sicily one thing above all is real: the Mafia.

RUN FOR
YOUR LIFE

PROLOGUE

Dear Hunter,

Today I have this crazy need to tell you what's going on with me.

Mamma's become a total wreck. It's not that she drinks or anything like that. But she has spells of anger and complaining, and I don't know what to do. She's shut herself up in the house for a month already. Because of her legs, she says. The fact is that she doesn't want to go out anymore. So I take care of most of the errands. Today I dragged Ilaria out so she wouldn't see the state Mamma was in. More and more often I have to take my sister out for a walk.

I know what you would tell me if we could talk face to face: that I'm safe and that's what matters, that as I get older things will straighten out. You'd be right, but it seems to me that this safety costs too much. It gets me depressed. I'm sorry, but tonight is one of those nights when I feel like smashing something. Or screaming dirty words.

I'm not crazy. I know you're as unreachable as a comic book character. But you're more real and important to me than the kids in school.

What kind of world is this, where we can't ever meet?

He doesn't sign it. There's no need to sign these letters. He takes the sheet of paper and folds it carefully into quarters. He gets an envelope and puts it in. On the envelope he writes simply, *To the Hunter.*

He bends down and takes out a small box of sailing gear from under the bed. He pokes around inside, adds the letter to the other envelopes, and arranges them at the bottom so that they're hidden. He closes the box and shoves it back under the bed.

PART I

Chapter 1
Santino

On Santino's fifth birthday, his father, Alfonso Cannetta, took him to Mondello, a beach resort near Palermo. They went in the car, just the two of them. Mamma and his grandparents stayed home in Tonduzzo with the flu.

The boy had never seen the ocean—or maybe he had, but when he was too small to remember it.

"Papi, can I go swimming?"

"It's too early to swim, Santù. The water is like ice. But I'll take you to a restaurant on the shore for pasta with sardines. You like that."

It was April. The sunlight spread over the sea like a gentle caress. The sand, millions of glistening grains, promised unknown sensations. Santino didn't know that the water could be bluer than his favorite marble.

They parked next to a clearing between the rocks, near a sailing club. Santino's eye was drawn to three young boys who were fiddling around with some small boats in front of a shed.

"Come on, let's go into the café. Aren't you thirsty?" his father said, shaking his head.

"Wait . . . ."

"What is it?"

He pointed. "Are they going out on the water?"

"You think those kids are doing all that work just to stay on the beach?"

"So let's wait."

Since it was Santino's birthday, he was the one to decide. They sat down on the steps of the rotunda to watch the kids more comfortably.

Three men arrived: the coaches.

A final sailor joined them, a boy of about twelve. He entered the shed and a couple of minutes later came out towing a dolly with a boat. The mast wasn't up yet.

The latecomer's maneuvers were precise to the millimeter, swift, without any slip-ups. *Click click* and the mast was up, *click click* and another part was up; Santino didn't know what it was called.

The boys were still rigging out their boats and the latecomer had already finished.

Santino's eyes stayed fixed on him.

The boy was thin, suntanned, his face alert, his black hair hanging over his forehead. Cool and calm, he waited patiently for the others. A prince.

Santino realized they were all finished when he saw them putting on life jackets over their wetsuits.

While his father was off getting something to drink, an old man dressed in white approached the small boy on the steps.

"I see that you like the Optimists. When you're eight years old, you should ask one of your parents to get you one. That's the minimum age, eight."

Optimist. It must be the name of the boats.

The man leaned toward him. "I can tell you, there's no better boat for a kid. It sails like a dream and never turns over."

Alfonso returned carrying two cans.

"Are you staying for the race?" asked the old man in white. "If you stay, you might want to sit on the edge of the dock. You can see better from there." He walked away with a friendly nod.

They went to the dock.

Very soon curious spectators were gathering from all directions. The Optimists were lowered from the dollies into the sea. The boys sat on the edge of the boats, leaning over so far that their backs were almost touching the water.

Santino kept his eye on his hero.

The boats all stopped at a certain distance from the shore. Three motorized lifeboats with the three trainers approached each of the waiting boats in turn.

The race began. Alfonso picked up his son and hoisted him onto his shoulders.

"I see him! It's him! He's the champion!" Santino shouted.

The man dressed in white appeared beside them. He was holding binoculars. "Want to have a look? The one with number 15 on his sail is going to win."

The old man turned toward Santino.

"You're such a *picciriddu*,* can you read the numbers?"

"No, he can't read them, this lazybones." Alfonso squeezed Santino's legs and he kicked against his father's chest in protest.

"Yes I can! It's that one there! The fastest!" He pointed to a speck out on the sea.

"Bravo! Lucio will win, I'm sure. At the end of the summer he'll be participating in the national races. That is, if he's still in Sicily. He only comes for the summer holidays."

Lucio. Now his favorite had a name.

"I can't see him anymore!" he cried.

"Try with these." The old man put the binoculars to his face. "Turn this little wheel until it comes into focus. Like this."

The minute he looked into the magic circle of the binoculars, Santino felt himself swept onto the small craft. He felt the wind on his face. The sprays of water. The taste of salt in his mouth. He was riding the waves, with Lucio. He was Lucio himself.

---

* *Picciriddu*: kid, in Sicilian dialect.

He felt the grip tighten on his ankles.

"Santino, stay still or you'll fall off me."

The old man beside them laughed.

"It's good to see this *picciriddu* show such enthusiasm," he said. "Register him in the Club when he's eight. It'll be a pleasure to coach him." He gently took the binoculars from Santino's hands. "Excuse me, I have to leave. Come to the awards ceremony, okay? You're invited!"

"But who won?" shouted Santino as his father took him down.

"Lucio. As usual," replied the man dressed in white as he walked away.

Chapter 2

Lucio

"Lucio, where are you?"

I fling open the bathroom door and face her.

"I'm here. I'm brushing my teeth, see?" I always have to show that I'm doing something necessary. Doing my own thing isn't appreciated.

"Hurry up. Illucia's ready."

Mamma bends down and gives my sister a quick kiss on her flushed cheeks.

I stare at Ilaria, flabbergasted.

Two enormous pink stuffed-animal ears rise from her head amid the clumps of black hair. Her velour sweater is pink, her tights are pink, her shoes are pink.

And I'm supposed to take her for a walk.

Ilaria struts around. A stubby little tail of a lighter pink is attached to her tights at the height of her behind.

"I'm not taking her out for a walk like that."

"Do you want her to stay shut up in the house? Take her to the Mascagni terrace near the sea. It'll be full of people in costumes. It's carnival."

"I'm not taking her there."

"So who will take her out, the *mischina*?"*

"Take her yourself!"

Mamma's legs are so swollen they look like an elephant's, so she doesn't go out anymore. It's been five months now.

"What?" she cries. "Aren't you ashamed of yourself!"

I step away and shout back at her. "I do the shopping, I pay the bills, I take Ilaria to preschool. I'm the only one in my class who never has a free moment. I'm only eleven years old!"

"Tell me, how come you used to be such a good boy, and now . . . ."

I can feel Ilaria looking at me. Her lips are puckered. Not for a kiss, but a bite.

"So, what is she dressed up as?" I shout.

"A bunny rabbit. Can't you see?"

I let out a groan. I feel sorry for my sister. I feel sorry for my mother. I feel sorry for myself. I feel sorry for the whole world.

I hold up my hand. "Okay. But tomorrow I'm going out on my own."

"Can I take my scooter?" Ilaria squeaks.

"Ask your brother."

---

* *Mischina*: poor thing, in Sicilian dialect.

Ask your brother. The message is clear: I'm the head of the family. As long as I take out the dorky bunny rabbit. As long as I do the shopping. As long as I'm there for her when she cries.

"Can I, Lucio? Can I?"

I shrug, gazing at this Disney cartoon character I have to call my sister.

"You can ride alone up to the terrace. Not where there's traffic. You get it, you silly goose? You have to do what I say all the time."

Mamma smiles. I hate that smile of hers when she gets what she wants.

As I put on my jacket I feel her warm breath on my neck, and she gives me a kiss.

"My little man."

I shake her off and open the door.

Outside, a cold wind hits us; the air is as blue as the sky, filled with multicolored confetti blowing up from the sidewalks. We head down Via Mazzini toward the ocean.

I hold my sister by the hand. I turn for a second to look at her. All winter her cheeks were like two red lights. Now they look like they're on fire.

We reach the big Mascagni terrace. I've always liked the rotunda facing the ocean, with its marble benches white as sugar.

I give Ilaria the scooter. "You see that empty bench? I'll be there."

14

I sit down, resigned. What I wouldn't give for a bike. Mamma says, you already have the Optimist, let's wait till your sister is a little older. Not that the boat is really mine, but at the boating club I use it all the same.

Ilaria's already dashed away. I gaze around at the crowded terrace.

Perched on the low wall is a girl in a mask. She has two gauze wings at her shoulders. A face like an angel. Her dress falls softly over her slender body. She rests a hand casually against a lamppost.

Below the wall three rowdy boys are talking to her. But she's looking at the sea and doesn't pay the slightest attention to them.

All of a sudden she lets go of the lamppost and jumps down just as one of the guys darts forward and leaps at her. They fall one on top of the other. The boy gets up. The angel, though, sits on the ground, bent over, holding her ankle. She takes off her mask and curses at the stupid boys, who quickly scatter.

Now she's looking around for a place to sit.

Here, here, I implore silently, staring down at the ground.

She gets up with difficulty and limps toward me.

She flops down on my bench. Without even a peek in my direction she bends over to massage her ankle.

I look her over secretly. Long, smooth blonde hair. But the thing that draws me to her perfect profile is the one eye I can see. It's pure blue.

"What a jerk that guy was!" I exclaim.

No reaction.

"I mean the one who made you fall," I say to her profile.

"Do you know him?" she asks, without turning around.

"No, but he seems like a bully."

With deliberate slowness, she finally turns her beautiful face toward me. The other eye is the same clear blue as the first. It's great to have a look at both of them.

She grimaces. "Damn him! I think I sprained my ankle."

"If you like I can walk you home."

"You don't have to."

"What are you? An angel?" I gesture with my chin at her back.

"No . . . . A dragonfly."

"A dragonfly." I add thoughtfully, "It figures."

"What figures? That I'm dressed as a dragonfly?" She looks at me like I'm some kind of weirdo.

I change the subject. "Where do you live?"

"Near Piazza della Repubblica."

"That's far from here. I'll take the bus with you."

The dragonfly looks around the terrace and gives a sharp whistle. A puppy comes running toward her.

"Ricky, here! Come over here!"

The dog, a brown and white mutt, runs to our bench and licks her hands, wagging his tail furiously. She holds him by his front paws and talks to him.

16

I have a feeling I'm not wanted. I suddenly remember Ilaria. I leap up from the bench and shout, "Ilaria! Ilaria!" Then she comes running toward us, her eyes on Ricky.

I turn toward the girl, who's playing with the dog.

"If you like, I'll see you home, if not, not. We're leaving now."

"Is that your sister?"

"Yes."

"What is she dressed as?"

"A pink bunny," I grunt.

Her lips ripple into a smile. "I don't even know your name."

"Lucio."

"I'm Monica."

Ilaria ducks down in front of the mutt to stroke him.

"Let's go," I announce. "We're going to take Monica and Ricky home."

Monica gets up. "I'll leave my bike here. It's chained up." She leans a hand on the arm I offer her.

The bus takes us downtown. From there, after a short walk, we go down the steps that lead to the Fosse Grande.*

The water of the canal reflects the houses, the stone footbridge, and the boats. Everything is doubled, quiet and dreamy.

"Here we are."

---

* Fosse Grande: one of the major canals in Livorno, where Lucio lives. (Leghorn, in English.)

Monica stops in front of a gate. She's already turned her back on us, her finger pressing the bell.

"So, *ciao*," I say, hiding my disappointment.

She turns back to us. "Would you do me a favor?"

"What?"

"Could you bring my bike back here? Tomorrow?" She puts a hand in her pocket and gives me the key, telling me where she left the bike. "I'll be waiting for you."

Chapter 3
Santino

Santino was running. Small, skinny, the only kid in short pants. He was just six and a half years old and his legs weren't as long as the other runners', who were eight.

And yet those little bare legs sliced through the air like propellers. His feet, in red Adidas sneakers, flew over the ground. The cold winter wind dried the sweat from his face.

He was in the lead. He pushed his chest forward and stretched out his arms; his hands were taut. He crossed the red ribbon of the finish line and dragged it behind him like the tail of a comet, still running, unable to stop. His father's wide open arms tackled him.

"Hey, where are you going? You were great! You left all the others in the dust!"

Santino's legs kept kicking for a few more seconds while he buried his head in his father's stomach. Deafened by the roar of his own blood, he took deep breaths. He couldn't speak.

Alfonso Cannetta detached him by lifting him up on his shoulders and carrying him in triumph past the audience, with everyone applauding.

"This is my son the champion! He'll end up in the Olympics!"

Santino felt strange, up there on his papa's shoulders, surrounded by all that applause. Euphoric, thrilled, but also strange. He tugged on Alfonso's hair to get him to quiet down.

His father persisted. "I'll make a champion out of him! You'll see!" he kept yelling. "I'll take him to the continent. To the big-time contests!"

It wasn't over yet. Santino gave up and simply sat on his father's shoulders. He was reminded of another awards ceremony. At the sea. The boy who won received a boat with a silver sail. Lucio, he was called. Even though Santino had never come across him since, he kept his image as sharp and clear as if he'd seen him yesterday.

After Lucio received his prize in the garden, Santino remembered, he had gone into the house to use the bathroom, and he had noticed a silver statuette on a table, a nude man seated with his knees bent and his arms stretched forward. A sailor. That same evening, at home, an odd thing happened. On his parents' double bed was one of Papa's undershirts, all rolled up and bulky. A tiny foot peeked out from the undershirt. The silver foot of the sailor. Later he took Papa over to the bed to show him, but the undershirt was empty. His father had laughed and said he must have been dreaming.

The applause had stopped. "Pa, put me down. No one's watching us anymore."

Alfonso looked around. The audience was now crowding around a table with snacks. He put his son down.

Someone turned toward them. "Come, come! What are you doing over there? Santinooo!"

Slowly, hand in hand, with big smiles pasted on their timid faces, they approached the table.

For a few minutes they were showered with congratulations. Your son is so great, where was he trained, and where did you get those red sneakers, are they the secret of his success? And so on, lots of smiles and pats on the back.

Alfonso, holding a glass of wine, got all worked up explaining that the shoes were bought in Palermo, the most expensive in the window because his son deserved the very best. He explained that he often drove him to the country and had him get out and run behind the car for miles. His son had good lungs.

A woman was staring at him, frowning. Santino's teacher.

"Yes, that's all very well. But Santino needs to come to school more often. If he studied the way he runs . . . ."

"Eh, my son doesn't like studying too much, I know because I was that way myself. Books . . . ." Alfonso shook his head vigorously. "Guys like us aren't made for the printed page."

"Without an education he won't get anywhere. Santino has to come to school." The woman lowered her glance to the boy with an ironic smile. "You're not made for books? That's too bad." She handed the prize to Santino. A small hardcover book.

Santino puzzled out the title aloud: "*His-tory of Sports Through the Cen-turies*. Cool! I'll read this one! Thanks!"

A little while later, Alfonso turned away from the crowd and sauntered off with his glass of wine. Santino didn't lose sight of him. His father, the wine still untouched, had stopped to study the bark of a tree. He seemed to be in a trance.

Santino left the buffet and his friends to go over to him.

"What are you looking at, Pa?"

Alfonso turned around, in a daze.

"Look at this," and he pointed to the wrinkled tree bark where tiny ants were walking up and down. "These ants," he said under his breath, "they know where they're going, they know what they're doing."

Santino was listening. It was as if his father had lit a match to illuminate his own dark and secret universe. A small flame that would last only a few seconds.

"They know the way . . ." Alfonso paused, drank his wine in one gulp, and turned to gaze absently at the crowd around the table.

"Maybe we should go," said Santino.

"Yes. Say hello to everyone for me tomorrow in school. Because tomorrow you're going to school."

Chapter 4
Lucio

I'm awake and basking in the dream I just had. No night-mares tonight, but a strange, sweet mirage: Monica and I are flying low over the water, which is covered with an expanse of wide black backs. Whales. We fly very close to them, totally unafraid.

The door opens slowly and Ilaria appears, dressed like yesterday.

From bed I shoot out a hand to chase her away and make a face like an ogre. "You want to see me all naked?"

She darts away.

At breakfast Mamma interferes again: I have to take Ilaria out with me.

I protest. "Yesterday you said I could go out by myself today."

"Me? I never said that!"

"You didn't say no, so it's the same as saying it's okay."

"She invited both of us," Ilaria shrieks. "Me and you!"

I cross my arms, stiff as a soldier.

"Illucia, *mischina*, what'll she do? All day Sunday in the house?"

"I have to return a bicycle to a friend who had an accident. *Illucia* can't come along."

I grab my jacket. Ilaria starts to cry.

"Monica said she'd be expecting us. She said *us*," she says between her sobs. "Both of us!"

Mamma leans against the door so I can't get out. "Won't you take her out just for an hour?"

"Take her yourself! And if your legs hurt too much to walk why don't you call a doctor? You're thirty-four years old and you look like fifty!"

"Can't you understand it's not something for a doctor? Someone cast a spell on me!"

"A spell? That's nuts!"

"Yes, a spell. You can laugh, but I need a *magara*,* not a doctor. Haven't you noticed I even talk like an alien?"

"An alien?"

"Yes. I hardly knew Italian and now I speak it very well. So!" She snaps her fingers. "I've heard of these cases. People under a spell start speaking a foreign language."

"But you speak Italian because we've been in Livorno for years."

---

* *Magara*: sorceress, witch doctor.

"So how do you explain that when I speak Italian I break out in a cold sweat?"

Anger surges inside me. "Cut it out with these superstitions!" I shout. "Call a doctor!"

Mamma seems to hollow out suddenly. She lowers her head and moves away from the door to let me pass. She opens it, just a crack. But it's an invitation.

Ilaria is having a full-fledged tantrum. They're both squawking together: two harpies.

I shut the door on them.

I run all the way to the Mascagni terrace, torn up by anxiety.

Mamma's flipped out. A spell! Speaking a foreign language! She'll never call a doctor, I know. If I called one, she'd refuse to go.

* * *

I find the bike exactly where Monica said it would be. In front, hooked onto the handlebars, is a big basket. That must be where she puts Ricky.

I get to the Fosse Grande in a flash. I carry the bike down the stairs leading to the canal, find the gate, and ring the bell.

The gate clicks and opens slightly. I chain the bike in the courtyard and go to the door where she disappeared yesterday. It's open, so I go in.

A voice calls from the top of the stairwell. I rush up and there she is.

She's holding Ricky in her arms. Smiling, she shows me the elaborate bandage on her left ankle. "What about Ilaria?"

"I wanted to come by myself. Here." I give her back the key to the padlock.

"Wait just a minute." She goes inside and a few minutes later reappears in a red parka, without Ricky. I can hear him barking from inside the apartment.

Good, I think. Puppies and bunny rabbits belong at home.

Monica leans on me, and we go down the stairs very slowly.

At the bottom, a few yards from the gate, is a bench facing the boats. We sit down.

"You're not from Livorno," she says. "Where are you from?"

"From Sicily, but we've been here several years—me, my mother, and my sister. Ilaria was born in Livorno."

"Oh, I get it."

Staring at the ships in the canal, I explain: "My father left a few years ago for Venezuela. He got a job on a farm near Caracas. We moved to Livorno because a cousin of Mamma's died and left us the apartment. Papa sends us money from Caracas. Mamma does embroidery for a factory here. She can embroider anything—bridal gowns, tablecloths . . . but she never makes enough money."

Monica listens without interrupting.

"Don't you miss your papa?" Monica asks in a low voice.

"I miss him a whole lot."

"Doesn't he ever come to see you?"

"The trip is too expensive." Then I shift to the offensive. I want to know all about her.

Monica's family is from Livorno, for generations. Her father is a lawyer, her mother a librarian. She takes dance classes but now she has to stop until her ankle is healed. She found Ricky last autumn on a beach in Ardenza.

"When I'm older I want to be a ballet dancer," she says, gazing at me with her blue eyes. "And you?"

"I like to race with the Optimists," I say. "Maybe in the future I'll be a captain. Last summer the *Livorno Courier* ran a photo of me after I won the Junior competition."

"Can I see it? Did you save the paper?"

"No."

"Why not?"

"I don't like to be photographed."

"I'd go wild if a newspaper had a photo of me dancing. Can you walk me back? I want to go home."

So there. I've bored her. I help her up from the bench. When we pass her bicycle I tell her it's fantastic.

At her door, she turns and hands me the key to the padlock. "Take the bike. You ride it—right now I have no use for it."

Chapter 5

Santino

Two days after the race a friend of his father's arrived in Tanduzzo: Pasquale.

He appeared at the Cannettas' doorstep with a new, shiny Kawasaki Z750. He was nineteen years old—young to have such a fancy motorcycle.

Perched on the seat, he seemed taller than he was: he had a long torso and short legs. His hair was reddish brown, his head small, his chin pointy. His eyes, sharp and spaced far apart, were like black pebbles. His hands flitted around in a girlish way, with white fingers and pale, manicured nails.

With that odd torso and his mustache, he reminded Santino of the stuffed weasel that sat on a shelf in the kitchen.

He'd known Pasquale for a while. Every so often he would turn up at their house, or else he and his papa would drive out to meet him, always in different places. The young man sometimes had a tic—when that happened, you had to pretend not to notice.

Alfonso wasn't home. Pasquale swore. He pushed his dark glasses up on his forehead.

"Tell your papa that I'll be waiting for him tomorrow evening at seven at Poggioreale Vecchia. Outside the gate. He's got to be there."

They were speaking at the door, not going in, because Pasquale didn't want to lose sight of the Kawasaki.

He turned back to Santino: "Repeat what I just told you."

"Tomorrow at seven at Poggioreale Vecchia. But that's the Ghost Town!"

"Smart *picciriddu*. You've got a head on your shoulders. Have you ever been there?"

"No. Papa says it's dangerous to walk inside."

"Don't worry. We'll meet outside at the gate."

He gave Santino's cheek a pinch. "Do you still have my amulet?"

Santino poked a hand inside his shirt and found the leather cord where the charm hung. He took it out to show Pasquale.

It was a *trinacria*,* the symbol of Sicily: a woman's round face with three bare legs radiating outward from it, knees bent. But this trinacria was different from all the others by a unique detail: instead of the face, there was

---

* *Trinacria*: ancient name for Sicily, meaning island of the three promontories.

a stamped design in yellow resin, and inside the resin, solitary and untouchable, was a wasp. You could see right away that it was a real wasp. Santino had often wondered if it had been placed in the boiling resin while it was still alive. It wasn't alive now—but encased inside, the insect looked immortal.

"Don't lose it. It'll bring you good luck, money, and women."

"Right." Santino started to put the charm back inside his sweater.

Pasquale stopped him. "Look. I have one, too." He took the amulet from beneath the starched collar of his shirt and put his next to Santino's.

"So far it's given me everything I wanted: money, women, everything. Sibilla made it specially for me. She's a very powerful *magara*."

The two charms were identical.

"I never take it off, not even when I sleep. I gave it to you because I'm your godfather, sort of."

Santino nodded, then, as if ashamed, he put the charm back inside his sweater.

Assunta's face peered out from inside.

"Ah, Pasquale. My husband isn't home," she said curtly.

"It's important that he come to our appointment tomorrow. I need to speak to him." He smoothed his gelled hair with his hand, tossed off a hasty goodbye, and lowered his dark glasses.

Santino watched him climb astride the Kawasaki. Pasquale seemed way too dressed up for a motorcycle. His outfit was more fitting for a funeral or a wedding: tie, black slacks, brilliantly shiny black shoes.

He must have money, he thought. Not like Papa. Pasquale must be the son of an important boss.

Santino hugged his mother, who'd come outside. He held her around the waist.

"Is he the one who finds work for Papa?" he asked.

Assunta made a face.

"Why don't you like Pasquale, Ma?"

"Because . . . he's not a good person." She hugged the boy tight, then picked him up and went back into the house.

* * *

The message was delivered. Alfonso's face darkened, then he shrugged his shoulders.

They were all sitting around the kitchen table, the warmest room in the small house: Mamma, Papa, Nonno Mico, who was Mamma's father, and his wife, Nonna Nunzia, an old woman who was not in the best of health.

"I told you things would get complicated," Nonno Mico remarked.

"He wants to talk to me, so what's the big deal?" Alfonso was looking down at his plate.

Assunta snapped, "You always think everything's so simple. That guy is bad news. They're mean people, dangerous."

"Cut it out! If it weren't for *u Taruccatu* there wouldn't be food on our plates tonight."

Santino was listening avidly. *U Taruccatu?*

"Just go, you have to go," said Nonno Mico.

"Of course I'll go!" Alfonso turned to his father-in-law. "I'm not afraid. I'll even take Santino."

Nonno Mico and Assunta looked at him in surprise.

"You think I would take him if it was dangerous?"

"Santino has school and also his catechism lesson. He has to prepare for his first communion!" Assunta burst out.

"He'll prepare another day." Alfonso was losing patience.

"Let me go, Mamma! I've already learned the catechism."

"You're not going anywhere!" His mother grabbed Santino and held him tight. He squirmed around to free himself, tears of humiliation in his eyes.

Nonno Mico raised a hand. "Assunta, stop being a mother hen. Santino is always hanging onto your apron strings like a baby."

"I am not," Santino shot back, trying to wriggle out of his mother's arms.

His grandfather ignored him. "Alfonso, take him along. It's a good idea."

There was silence in the kitchen. Reluctantly, Assunta opened her arms and released Santino. The boy ran to his grandfather. The old man always had the last word. No one would ever have dared to oppose his decision.

*   *   *

To be sure to reach Poggioreale Vecchia, the Ghost Town, on time, they started out at five in the morning. The day was dismal: it was raining and the low sky resembled a mass of molten lead. The rain veiled the countryside, which was still very dry.

Despite the overcast day, Santino was all revved up. He and Papa alone in the car—that was as good as it gets.

"Pa, what is Poggioreale like?"

"Old Poggioreale is a town completely in ruins. There was an earthquake. No one lives there anymore. But the facades of the houses are still standing." He looked at his son. "They'll collapse if anyone breathes on them," he added, in the hushed tones of someone telling a fairy tale about ogres.

Santino laughed.

"Once upon a time you could go there in a truck and carry off chunks of balconies, marble coats of arms, doors." Alfonso described these things so well that Santino could visualize them. "Heavy stuff. Stuff foreign tourists would give plenty of dollars for."

"Did they steal them?" Santino asked.

"Well . . . . Because of that the cops put up a gate; they left only two footpaths. So, if you're on foot, what can you carry off? A brick!"

"Are we going in?"

"No."

"Why not?"

"We have to stay in the middle of the road so rocks don't fall on our heads, and I don't trust you—you're a wild pony."

"No, I'm not!"

"Oh no?"

They were silent for a few minutes. The rain cascaded around the car.

"Pa," Santino asked, "Who is *u Taruccatu?*"

Alfonso laughed. "That's who we're going to meet."

"Do I know him?"

"Of course!"

"Isn't he called Pasquale?"

"Don't you know that we give everyone nicknames?"

Santino's eyes lit up. "When I think of him, I call him Weasel. Like the one we have in the kitchen."

His father laughed again. "Yes, he does look like our weasel. But we rebaptized him *u Taruccatu* because he's so superstitious. He even believes in the magic of tarot cards."

"So I'll call him that too. *U Taruccatu.*"

"Don't let him hear you . . . ."

"I would never do that."

Alfonso turned toward his son. "Let's see if you can guess: which of my friends is called *Steccasicca*?"*

Santino thought about it. He didn't know all his father's friends. He took a guess.

"Alberto?"

"Wrong! Who walks like he has a stick up his . . . ?"

"Giuseppe!"

"Right! And who is *u Surciu*?"**

"Alberto?"

"Very good. And *u Curtu*?"***

The game went on for a good stretch of road. Santino had never felt so close with his father.

"Pa, what do they call you?"

Alfonso turned to him and, keeping his hands on the steering wheel, bent his head to brush his lips against Santino's ear. He uttered a word.

Santino stared wide-eyed in admiration.

"That's what they call you?"

"Righto."

"Why?"

"Maybe because of my great intelligence," Alfonso replied, nuzzling his hair.

They laughed together.

---

* *Steccasicca*: dry stick.
** *u Surciu*: fat rat.
*** *u Curtu*: Shorty.

When they reached the gate that enclosed the ruins of Poggioreale Vecchia, Santino immediately spied Pasquale's Kawasaki parked on the deserted piazza.

"You stay in here," Alfonso said. "Don't leave the car for any reason."

The rain had almost stopped.

Santino nodded, cowed by the abrupt bossy tone that shattered the warm closeness of the trip.

Alfonso got out and stood waiting next to the car. The motorcycle was there but *u Taruccatu* was nowhere to be seen.

A few minutes later Santino caught sight of him beyond the gate, on the central road of the Ghost Town. He came toward them, the dark glasses hiding his eyes.

Alfonso left the car and went to meet him. They began talking on the piazza. Santino couldn't hear them, so he opened the window. That was better, even if the cold froze his nose.

U Taruccatu was complaining about their being late.

"Why did you go into the Ghost Town?" Alfonso interrupted.

"I had to take a piss."

"Why did you make me come all this way? Do you have a job for me?"

U Taruccatu's expression changed. His mustache started to quiver. He was suddenly in a rage.

"You scoundrel! Did you think we wouldn't find out what you did? I already warned you." He was yelling and trembling all over. "My father didn't like your cheating one bit. I had to defend you, you who . . . ." He finished this speech by bringing his hands to his chest to form an X with his index fingers crossed and pointing down.

Santino recognized this gesture. It meant that his father was a fool. He kept listening, growing more and more worried.

His father seemed ill at ease. "I didn't think . . . . Just for a few *picciuli* . . . a pitiful amount."

Pasquale was seized by his tic. He spat when he talked.

"The owner of the warehouse paid us protection money regularly! And you, you wretched idiot, you walked away with that truckload! Moron! I can't protect you anymore."

Santino was shocked. They didn't seem like the same people. Not even his father—he was acting meek, apologizing, keeping his eyes lowered.

"Give me some other job," he was saying to the young man. "Even if it's risky . . . ."

"You're in disgrace, don't you get it? You have to wait. That's why I sent for you, to warn you not to act like an imbecile again. There'll be work when we say so."

"But what will I do? You know I have a family."

"That's your problem. And make sure not to step out of line again."

Pasquale walked away from Alfonso and got on his Kawasaki. Only at that moment did he notice Santino in the car.

The boy suffered the cold impersonal glare of those black eyes trained on him.

U Taruccatu spit on the ground and started the motor with a din. An instant later he was far away.

On the trip home father and son didn't exchange a single word.

Chapter 6
Lucio

In the morning Ilaria is still sulky about yesterday. We walk to her preschool in silence.

"I didn't get to play with Ricky either," I say to break the ice.

"So what? Mamma said that if you keep on this way she'll send you back to the therapist."

"I'm the one who decides if I want to see the therapist."

"Mamma said she can't handle you anymore. If you keep it up she'll send you to her. She'll make you go."

"It's not a punishment, you know."

"No?"

I laugh in her face. "No. I liked going there."

"What's a therapist?" she asks crossly.

"Someone who . . . who wants you to tell her things."

"What things?"

Ilaria knows nothing about when I was little and saw Dr. Gaetani twice a week. She had me make drawings. I told her my nightmares. She never scolded or criticized. But now that I'm older I can manage on my own. Dr. Gaetani is part of a phase I don't really want to think about.

"Stop it," I tell her. "You're bugging me."

"Do only bad people go to therapists?"

I give her a serious look. "Do you think I'm bad, Ilaria?"

"Sometimes."

"And now?"

"Now not so much. But if you weren't bad, why did you go there?"

"Because I was sad that Papa had left for Venezuela. I missed him. I still miss him."

"Did I ever see Papa?"

"No. You were born after he left."

"There's not even a photo of him in the house."

"I know . . . ."

Ilaria stops short on the sidewalk. In front of us a gray cat is stretched out on the ground. It's in a weird position, disjointed. I don't see any wounds. We go a few feet closer, then I freeze. I tug Ilaria's hand to keep her back.

"It's dead," I say.

"It died yesterday," Ilaria murmurs slowly in a faint voice.

"Why yesterday? It probably died this morning, otherwise someone would have taken it away already."

"No. Yesterday." She stares at the cat. "Yesterday," she repeats stubbornly.

"Okay, let's go, it's getting late."

I drag her along. It's useless arguing with Ilaria.

We move on, skirting the small corpse. She walks along reluctantly and repeats to herself: "No one will die today." She seems to want to convince herself, seeing that she couldn't convince me.

"Here we are. *Ciao*."

Ilaria sets out alone toward the front door of the preschool.

I run toward my school. In class I sit in my usual place, next to Marco, a friendly easygoing geek. I can copy off him with no problem. We probably exchange half a dozen words all day.

I don't speak much to the others either. I like it that way. They're all pretty childish.

But Monica, no, she's different.

*   *   *

I shop at the central market because you can find everything there. I go with Ilaria on Saturday afternoons. She likes it because I always buy her candy or a plastic toy.

The market feels like an immense nineteenth-century station. It has different rooms and the ceiling is very high, with a skylight made of iron and glass. The stalls with all their goods on display are arranged in aisles, which are crowded with people bumping and jostling as they walk back and forth. I hold Ilaria's wrist so I don't lose her. The more she tries to wriggle away, the tighter I hold her.

Mamma counted out the *picciuli* she gave me (she still uses that Sicilian word for money). We walk around a while looking for the least expensive vegetables. For fish I go to Carmelo the Sicilian's stall. Sometimes he gives me *paranza*, which are small fish full of bones. You can use them to make a soup called *cacciucco*.

Today, next to Carmelo there's a buxom dark-haired woman with big teeth and a black shawl. I've never seen her before.

"This is Gina," says Carmelo. "She came from Sicily to give me a hand. I've got some *ragni*, so fresh they're almost alive. Do you want some?"

Ragni are ordinary fish. I think when they're alive they sting, which is why they're called that.* They're very cheap.

"How come your Mamma sends two *picciriddi* like you to do the shopping?" Gina asks.

Carmelo tosses three big *ragni* onto the scale. "Their mother's not well."

I nod silently.

"*Mischina* . . . . What's wrong with her?"

---

* *Ragni*: spiders.

42

"Her legs," I answer reluctantly.

Carmelo cries out as if a light had gone on in his head. "My cousin is a *ciarmavermi.** Gina, could you help their mother, what do you think?"

I know what a *ciarmavermi* is. It's a witch doctor, a level below a *magara*. A quack, good for gullible people like my mother.

"I don't think so," I mumble.

Gina gazes at me for a moment, then loses interest and turns toward another customer.

I pay and we leave with the bag of *ragni*. It's heavy. Carmelo must have added the *paranza*. All we need is fruit and vegetables and we can go home.

"What's a *ciarmavermi*?"

I look down at Ilaria. "Someone who says they can pull your sickness out of you."

"Can they take worms out of your stomach?"

"Oh, come on!"

Ilaria thinks this over; she's so busy thinking that she forgets to ask me to buy her candy. But I get her a huge rainbow lollipop anyway. Before I hand it over, I tell her: "Don't tell Mamma about that woman, okay?"

She stares at me as if I've suddenly become transparent, then looks down at the lollipop I'm still holding.

"Okay?" I repeat more sharply.

---

* *Vermi*: worms.

"Okay." She seizes the lollipop and spins it around in her fingers.

*   *   *

At home, once the groceries are put away, I turn on the TV. It's time for the news, which I watch all the time. At school they tell us to pay attention to the world news. I've explained this again and again to Mamma and Ilaria, who are annoyed by my puzzling habit.

After the news, I shut myself up in my room to do my homework.

Half an hour later the door suddenly bursts open. Mamma has a peculiar look on her face.

"Lucio, I found out from Ilaria that at the market you met a *ciarmavermi*. Why didn't you tell me?"

"I've asked you a thousand times to knock!"

"You know how much I want to find a *magara*."

"I didn't tell you because you wouldn't be able to go to the market."

"You could ask her to come here. Tomorrow, go ask her if she would come to our house. I'm ready to pay whatever she wants. Insist!"

I don't say anything. I can't think of any way to refuse.

"Maybe she could lift the spell. Bring her here, please! If she won't come, I can take a taxi to the market."

The only taxi Mamma ever took in her life was the one to the hospital when Ilaria was born.

I nod. "Okay, tomorrow I'll go look for her."

Mamma takes my hand and gazes at me. "You're the best son in the world. I'm lucky to have you."

She says it in Sicilian, a weighty assertion, as if it were a sacred truth, the one truth that could save us all.

Chapter 7
Santino

Day after day, the food that appeared on the Cannettas' table dwindled down to pasta and beans, bread with olives and onions, plus some unripe tomatoes stolen from a neighbor's garden.

When hunger became urgent, Nonno Mico winked at the kitchen shelf where three books were kept: a farming manual, a *Lives of the Saints*, and the book on sports that Santino had won. Next to the books was Nonno Mico's stuffed weasel. Standing upright, it showed the long white stripe of fur on its stomach.

"What do you say, Assunta? Is it time to cook it?"

"Come on, it would stink!"

"If it stinks, it stinks. It'll taste like chicken!"

The joke was repeated over and over. The weasel was Nonno's pride and joy: he had shot it when he was thirteen because it was killing chickens. Nonno's father was so proud of his son, he had it stuffed.

The walls of the house gave off an icy dampness. Santino went to school willingly because the classrooms were heated.

Alfonso disappeared for days at a time and returned looking despondent, with a bunch of wild chicory. Santino hadn't seen him smile since the day when they went together to meet *u Taruccatu.*

Mamma was worried about her son's first communion. Since he wasn't yet seven, Santino should have waited till he was older before making his first communion. There was one hitch, though: Don Vittorio, the priest who was considered a kind of patron saint throughout Palermo, should have conducted the ceremony, but he already had one foot in the grave. In his youth he had been the parish priest of Tonduzzo. He had officiated at all the baptisms, first communions, and weddings of the entire Cannetta family. Now, over ninety, he lived in Palermo. Rumor had it that he wouldn't last long.

So, to be sure that Santino followed in the family tradition, they had to work fast.

Assunta was planning to celebrate the great occasion: she wanted to invite distant relatives and friends to a fine country restaurant, but without *picciuli* the plan was impossible. And there was hardly any money in the house.

It wasn't total poverty, but close to it.

One evening, Alfonso came home in a different mood. He tossed some bills on the table.

"I found work," he announced.

"And they already paid you?" Assunta asked, astonished.

"I asked for an advance."

She scrutinized her husband for a long time, tightening her lips. She counted the money. "It's not much. Not even enough for the band."

"It's only an advance," her husband repeated.

As usual, they were all in the kitchen. Santino noted his father's poker face. He didn't understand any of it. He should have been cheerful again, shouldn't he?

With a sullen expression, Assunta gathered the money from the table and left the room to put it in a safe place.

Nonno Mico confronted his son-in-law. "What work did you find?"

"Trucking. They gave me a truck to use."

"What kind of trucking?"

Alfonso said nothing, but didn't take his eyes off his father-in-law.

"I get it. Stolen goods," Nonno Mico remarked dryly.

"Stolen . . . stolen. That's none of my business. All I have to do is carry the shipment to the port of Messina."

"Make sure you don't cheat Don Ciccio. You've already seen what happens with his precious son and heir."

Santino understood that Don Ciccio's son was Pasquale, *u Taruccatu*. That explained the huge Kawasaki and the swanky clothes.

"That one talks and talks, trying to scare me. Me! I'm no coward," his papa replied. "I'm not afraid because *u Taruccatu* is not a man of action."

Nonno Mico shook his head. "Are you sure the family who hired you is on good terms with Don Ciccio?"

"Yes, I'm sure. They don't pay protection money to anyone."

"You couldn't find any other work?" Nonno Mico asked again.

"No, they didn't need me anywhere."

* * *

A month passed and the cold in the Tonduzzo hills didn't let up. There was always a harsh wind that swept away the clouds. The sky was as blue as the Virgin's robe.

Santino's communion was drawing near. The parish of Tonduzzo guaranteed the outfit for the ceremony; the little church of San Cataldo in Palermo supplied the flowers in honor of Don Vittorio. All they needed was money for the feast. Assunta had her eye on a tourist place with a vegetable garden in the country, not far from Palermo. But what money they had barely covered daily life for the five members of the Cannetta family. Even paying for Nonna Nunzia's false teeth had been put off until better times.

Assunta felt sick at the idea of giving up the dinner. Just to reserve the restaurant she had stooped to asking for loans from everyone she knew. She'd gotten a good number of excuses and apologies, but no money had come out of any pockets. She even took the bus to Salemi on her own to consult a *magara* she knew who gave her advice. She said the dinner had to be held at all costs, for at least fifty people. The Host offered from Don Vittorio's hands would be doubly holy. The feast would keep evil spirits far from the *picciriddu*. She had to serve the evil spirits too: at the very least three extra table settings. They should be served first, with the best morsels. Without a big dinner, the ceremony could end in a misfortune.

Santino tried to tell his Mamma that he didn't want a big party. But Assunta stuck to her guns: it was a social duty, it brought honor to the family. And besides, the *magara* predicted bad luck for all of them if they didn't hold a real banquet.

Alfonso was away for several days, busy with the trucking business. But as soon as he returned home, his wife started to fret about the communion.

"Let's forget the dinner," Alfonso said gloomily one evening.

Nonna Nunzia shook her head. "The dinner? What dinner?"

They explained the whole thing to her again.

"You can do it here in the kitchen!" And she laughed.

"Without a real dinner in a proper place, no communion." Assunta kept quiet about the three extra place settings for the evil spirits.

Nonno Mico, who'd been silent up to this moment, studied the family members one by one. When he was certain of their attention, he made his announcement.

"It means I'll be looking for work too."

A shocked silence. Santino's grandfather had a lean body and large, knobby hands, but he was old, his joints ached, his lungs were bad, and he coughed a lot. What kind of work could he find?

The old man chuckled as he watched the stunned faces around him. "You think just because I'm an old man I can't help the family?" He put his hands together and linked his pinkies, winking at Alfonso.

Santino didn't miss that look of complicity between his father and grandfather. Those two had an understanding, like partners.

A week before the date set for Santino's communion, Nonno Mico and Alfonso left the house together early in the morning. They returned late at night. The following day Assunta found on the table enough *picciuli* to rent the restaurant for the party. It might even be enough for Nonna Nunzia's false teeth. How they had managed to make the money appear wasn't her business. She convinced herself it was because of the *magara* in Salemi. Besides, whatever her father and her husband cooked up between themselves, they did it for the family, for the *picciriddu*, so it must be a good thing.

These were happy days. Papa and Mamma had cheerful smiles and were unusually affectionate with each other. They let Santino sneak in between the two of them in a hug, like making a sandwich—they were the bread and he was the little cheese tucked in the middle.

51

Chapter 8
Lucio

I told Mamma that after all my pleading, Rita the witch doctor had agreed to come over next Sunday, and now Mamma lets me do whatever I want.

I hang out with Monica. We have long talks. She tells me about films and I tell her all the juicy gossip I've heard on the news.

At the bit about the packs of wild dogs that come into Sicilian cities at night to maul children and adults, her eyes get wide.

Monica isn't keen on having me go in her house—I understand that, so I don't ask about it. I go to meet her and stay outside the door while she puts on her jacket. Then we go downstairs together. I help her on the stairs, but there's really no need anymore—her ankle is almost all better.

Monica is the first girl I've been close to in Livorno (Mamma doesn't count because she's too old, and Ilaria is too young).

If I think about the time when her ankle will be completely healed and she can return to her dance classes, I'm flooded with doubt. She won't have any more time for me. She'll want her bike back.

But that moment hasn't come yet, and meanwhile I'm pedaling toward her house.

"I came today because I can't tomorrow," I announce as we go to sit down on the bench.

"How come?"

"On Sunday Mamma will have a visitor. I'll have to take care of Ilaria."

"So bring your sister."

How can I tell her I don't want to leave Mamma alone with the *ciarmavermi*, not even for a minute?

"What is it, Lucio?"

My face gets serious. By now it's an automatic reflex. My long face, and Monica giggles.

I look at her mouth, soft and full, at her eyes fixed on me like a penetrating azure glow. I don't know which I like better, her eyes or her lips. Her nose is beautiful too.

"There's something, I can feel it," she says firmly.

I'm surprised and a little anxious as I hear myself telling her about Mamma's obsession with magic. I describe the *ciarmavermi* I met at the market, a fraud for sure.

I explain what *magaras* are in Sicily. There it wouldn't seem strange for Mamma to consult one, but we're in Livorno now and . . . .

53

This longing to confide in her is pushing me to reveal family secrets. Who knows where I'll stop?

"But a *ciarmavermi* isn't as powerful as a *magara*. She can't do really serious harm," I add.

"So you believe in it too?"

"Give me a break! It makes me mad because this witch doctor will cost us a lot. And we don't have enough to . . . ."

Monica interrupts me. "I believe magic can help. If you believe in it, of course."

I look at her, amazed.

"Here in Livorno, lots of people make a vow to the Madonna in the shrine of Montenero. They say she performs miracles. Have you ever been to the shrine?"

I shake my head, still amazed.

"In my opinion," Monica continues, "these miracles are not so different from those of the Sicilian *magaras*. My father and mother are atheists. My papa says everyone has the right to believe in whatever they want, and that if a person is Catholic they shouldn't go around judging others' beliefs."

"Are you an atheist too?"

She thinks it over. A small wrinkle I haven't seen before appears in the middle of her brow.

"I don't know . . . . I have to tell you something, Lucio," she says, raising her head.

My heart is pounding.

"I have . . . a little brother who's one year old. Duccio. I haven't spoken about him till now because . . . ."

She stops. Her lips are trembling. "Duccio was very premature," she continues in a whisper. "Too soon." She pulls herself together, and the whisper becomes a faint voice, very emotional. "They had him in an incubator for a long time, then he came home."

"Ilaria was two months premature also!" I cry, excited by the coincidence. "She was in an incubator too!"

Monica raises a hand to tone down my enthusiasm.

"Your sister is healthy as a horse. But Duccio . . . they found out he was sick. He has a serious illness."

"What does he have?"

"Epilepsy. He's already had seizures. And so little!"

"I'm sorry. I'm so sorry."

Monica looks at me intently. "The secret is that I made a vow to the Madonna of Montenero."

"You did?" I respond a bit foolishly.

"If Duccio gets better I'll donate an *ex voto** to the shrine, one of those four little paintings, and also I'll give up . . . maybe I'll give up . . . ."

I put my arm around Monica. She leans her head on my shoulder.

"What will you give up?"

"Dancing."

---

* *Ex voto*: a gift to the church offered by Catholics in gratitude for answered prayers.

"Oh, no! No! No!"

That was an idiotic response: if she gave up dancing it could mean that her little brother would be cured, and here I'm saying No, no, no, to a miraculous thing.

Monica jerks up. She wipes her wet nose with the back of her hand and looks at me with teary eyes that are full of defiance.

"My problem is, I have a feeling this vow occurred to me for a selfish reason."

"What do you mean?"

"I think I'm starting to get fed up with dance classes. You're the only one I'm telling this to."

"So what's the problem?"

"Don't you see? Maybe I made the vow to have an excuse to drop the classes. If that's true, then the vow isn't worth a damn and I'm just a petty person."

"No! No, you're not! It's not your fault if you're fed up with dancing. You'll see, your brother will get better even without your vow."

She lowers her head. "I wish so much that he would get better." She passes her hand over her face. "Now I've told you everything. Your turn."

"My turn?"

"I told you things I haven't told any other person. Now you have to do the same."

I pull away from her, stand up, and turn away. "My secret is that I have no secrets," I declare, facing the boats.

"That's a lie."

"You're saying I'm a liar?"

"Yes."

"If I say you're right, that I'm a liar, that means I'm not." I speak without turning around.

Behind me is silence. Then an impatient puff of breath. At last I hear her irritated voice. "I know those games too. You made me talk, but now that it's your turn . . . ."

I turn toward her. "I made you talk? Me?"

I don't want to argue, but since she doesn't answer, I announce that it's time for me to go home.

Monica gets up from the bench without a word. She stubbornly avoids my eyes. We go upstairs in silence.

The door is open. Monica enters. I want her to look at me again. Even if she laughs, I don't want her to disappear this way.

"I do have one thing I haven't told anyone."

She spins around.

I speak hastily. "I have a secret friend. I call him the Hunter."

"Who is he?"

"I can't tell you."

"Oh, really. And when do you see him?"

"We can't see each other."

Monica raises her eyes to the sky.

"That's pathetic," she says softly as she closes the door in my face.

Chapter 9
Santino

He put on his red shoes. It was the third pair Papa had bought him, always the same Adidas. His feet were growing, and he needed good shoes for running.

It took all of Mico's authority to convince Assunta to let her son go with them. The ceremony of his first communion and the lunch were the next day.

As they were gathered at the doorstep, ready to leave, Assunta asked, in a petulant tone, "Can you give me a lift to the country inn? I have to choose the songs for the band, and pick out the flowers . . . ."

"What about your mother?" Alfonso interrupted. "You're going to leave her alone in the house?"

"I can use the *picciriddu* here to help out. He can keep her company."

Santino bent his head and stared at his shoes. Papa had promised that on the way back he could run behind the car to show his grandfather how fast he was.

"Nunzia can manage fine on her own." Nonno Mico raised his voice. "Right, Nunzietta?"

The old woman laughed with her toothless mouth. "Go, go, I'll take a little nap."

Assunta got into the car in the back seat next to her son. She got out at the tourist inn, a pretty cottage out in the countryside with a courtyard and orchards.

"We'll come to pick you up around five thirty," Alfonso called out.

They left without another word. Not a breath, just silence. Too silent for Santino.

No one had told him why they had to return to the Ghost Town. He recalled uneasily the ugly scene between Papa and Pasquale. Since that day he hadn't seen the young man with the Kawasaki. It was better that way. He didn't like him anymore. He thought of taking off the charm he'd given him, but he always forgot. He had it around his neck right now. He'd get rid of it as soon as he could.

The silence was grating on his nerves. He couldn't take it anymore. He fidgeted around on the back seat. "Papa," he blurted out. "What are we going to do in the Ghost Town?"

Alfonso didn't answer. Nonno Mico spoke, turning around to look Santino in the eye.

"An important matter. We have to give back some money."

"What money?" Santino asked.

"The money for the party. The *picciuli* we brought home the other day."

"What about Mamma? What does she say about it?"

"Mamma doesn't know," Alfonso replied in a low voice. "We'll tell her when we get back."

Santino's throat tightened with apprehension. "She put it away in a safe place . . . ."

"And we took it. If we'd asked her for it, who knows what kind of a fuss . . . ."

"But then . . . how will she pay for the dinner?"

"There's not going to be any dinner. There can't be. You have to understand, Santù; there are more important things than a dinner. This money has to be returned today."

His grandfather turned back around and Santino collapsed against the seat. More than disappointed, he felt shaken, confused. They had tricked his mother, they had left her at the inn all involved in planning the party and choosing the flowers, and now there wouldn't be any party.

"What about all the guests?" Santino asked. "Uncle Turi and all the others?" For an instant he thought of the gifts that would vanish along with the guests.

"Don't you worry about it—they'll think up some reason. We'll have something at home, we can use the neighbors' garden. And then . . . ." His grandfather turned to Santino again. "There's still a slight chance that we might keep the money for a while. We have to see if *u Taruccatu* is willing to talk about it. That's why we didn't say anything to Mamma. It might just happen that tonight we'll bring her *picciuli* back safe and sound. We'll put it back where it was."

"Oh, good!" Santino leaned his elbows on the back of the front seat to be closer to Papa and Nonno. "So then Mamma won't notice anything."

"Remember, it's a very slim chance."

"How slim?"

"About like a flea."

"That tiny? But . . . why do we have to give it back?"

"Your Papa and I made a mistake."

"Mico, why are you telling him . . . ." interrupted Alfonso, who had been silent till then.

Mico didn't let him finish. "Your son ought to know; he should learn from our errors. And he'd find out soon anyhow. Let me finish."

"It's not something a *picciriddu* can understand . . . ."

"He can too understand. Look, Santino, a week ago we took some of the stolen goods we were supposed to deliver off the truck. Televisions and computers, brand new."

"You stole them?"

"Don't act so shocked. Come on, you know it was the only way we could get by."

Santino thought it over. He knew, but he didn't want to hear his Nonno say it out loud. That made it all too real.

"It was already stolen goods," his grandfather went on. "We simply took it away from the thieves and resold it to a friend of mine who gave us ready cash."

61

"So it's not really stealing?" Santino asked weakly.

"That's not the point. It was our bad luck that we didn't know the trucking business belongs to the Zolfatari family." Still looking at him, Mico explained. "It's a syndicate that's an enemy of Don Ciccio's clan. Now they'll think that the Don gave the order. Don Ciccio took this all very badly, because he doesn't want a war with the Zolfataris just now."

"So?" the child murmured.

"So, to make them pardon this mistake, we have to give Pasquale back all the money we earned. He'll give it to his father, who'll give it to the Zolfataris as a peace offering. Do you understand?"

Santino screwed up his face in misery.

His grandfather smiled. "Don't cry. Keep your tears for later. Before we give back the *picciuli* we'll ask *u Taruccatu* to give us some more time. If he insists, though, we'll have to hand it over on the spot. Can you figure out why we brought you with us?"

"Not really," Santino replied.

"Because that money was for your communion with Don Vittorio. We'll explain that to Pasquale. It's something he can understand, he's a devout Christian. If he sees you're disappointed, all weepy, if you also beg and plead a little, he might let it go. He's rolling in dough."

"I don't care about the dinner!" Santino cried. "I don't need the presents."

Tears of rage sprang to his eyes.

"Your Mamma cares. Isn't that enough?"

Santino fell back in the seat. He was miserable. Furious. He kept his face stubbornly glued to the window.

The landscape looked the same as the time before: winter hadn't yet loosened its grip; the ground was still hardened by ice. He recognized the outline of a hill that looked like a woman's breast. When they'd gone along this road the last time, he'd noticed the puffy shape of the hills just before they arrived.

"I'll throw that charm in *u Taruccatu*'s face. I'll spit on him," he muttered against the window pane.

"What did you say?" His grandfather turned to him. "What'll you do?"

"Nothing. Nothing."

Nonno Mico stretched out his hand to give him a pinch. "That's a good boy. *He who spits on a Christian dies like a dog*. Remember that."

Chapter 10

Lucio

Sunday. The appointment with the witch doctor is for three thirty. For an hour now, Mamma's been wandering around the house, stopping to lean on the furniture, like a crazy bluebottle fly.

Besides the living room, our apartment has two bedrooms: I'm in the smaller one, and Mamma and Ilaria sleep in the big double bed in the other room.

The downstairs buzzer rings. As she gets up to answer, Mamma makes a gesture with her hands that's unmistakable. It means: Get lost! I drag Ilaria into my room and close the door.

We stand in the middle of my room, crammed with all my things. The shelves on the walls are filled with schoolbooks and trophies I won with the Optimist: miniature boats and plaques.

We stare at each other in a tense silence, our ears keen for sounds from the living room. The voices are muffled.

"I brought the candles. And a crucifix, the playing cards, and an olive branch."

"Please come in this room and sit down, if you don't mind the bed. It's more private."

The creaking sound of a door opening and closing. Then nothing more.

Ilaria is the first to get tired of standing there in silence, eavesdropping.

"Play with me," she commands.

"What?"

"Let's play with Barbie. She goes shopping."

"I don't feel like it."

"Then let's play school. You're the pupil and I'm the teacher. You have to recite a poem."

"What poem?"

"*Pin Pirulin.*"

"I don't know that one." I'd like to tiptoe out to listen at Mamma's bedroom door.

"Yes you do. *Pin Pirulin was crying. He wanted half an apple . . . .*"

I interrupted. "Look, be good and stay here for five minutes?"

"You have to recite the poem! Where are you going?"

"Out there. You know who that woman is? She's a witch." I make a face like I'm under a spell and fall down on the bed. The next second, Ilaria is sitting next to me.

"Does she have a magic wand?"

"Sure. Maybe she'll cure her."

A shiver runs up and down my sister's body. Her eyes are gleaming with excitement.

"How?"

"She'll tap her legs with her magic wand."

"And then Mamma will walk?"

"Mamma will run and chase you!" I grab her by the shoulders to tickle her.

"Will the witch make Papa come back from Venezuela?" she asks between giggles and squeaks.

"Papa isn't in Venezuela," I answer, moving away from her.

Her eyes grow large and dark as wells. Her red cheeks are glowing.

"No, that's a lie," she says slowly. "Our Papa is in Venezuela and sends us money."

"That's what they told you. But I know the truth. He's in Russia."

My orders are to keep Ilaria occupied at any cost. To keep her in here. So I have the right to say whatever I want.

"In . . . Russia?"

"Yes."

"Where is Russia?"

"Far away."

"Why is he there?"

"Bad men kidnapped him. Russian spies."

I can almost see the little wheels turning in her head. "So then who sends us money?" she asks defiantly.

66

"A friend of Papa's who's in Venezuela."

"Why?"

"Because he cares about him. Papa is a great scientist, but very few people know that. A long time ago he invented a very powerful formula and the spies think he might still have it."

"A formula?"

"Yes. I'll show you. I have it. He gave it to me for safe-keeping before you were born."

I get my backpack, click open the lock, and take out my math notebook. I very carefully take out a sheet of paper folded in quarters and open it slowly. There's writing above the numbers.

"Look!" I hold it out to Ilaria, who takes it hesitantly.

"This is what they're looking for." I tap my finger on the paper she's gripping tightly. "With this formula you can . . . ."

Ilaria is holding her breath. She studies the paper, wrinkles her brow.

"You can . . . . Well, you've seen what ants can do, right?"

"What do they do?"

Her eyes are two solar eclipses. If I keep on talking they'll swallow up her nose and mouth. Ilaria will disappear and only her eyes will remain, lit up and roaming around the room.

"One single ant can carry on its back a crumb that weighs a hundred times its body weight. Everyone knows that."

"I didn't know," murmurs Ilaria.

"Naturally, you're still a little girl. But Papa, who has a scientific mind, had a brilliant idea."

"What idea?"

"To extract the liquid from the ants' bodies, mix it with a combination of poison ivy, cherry flavor, and some glue." Again I tap my hand on the piece of paper. "This is the formula for the glue—the measurements of the ingredients have to be exact, otherwise it won't work."

"So then?"

"Then you have to drink it. Whoever drinks a glass of this juice just once a day, after a week will have the strength of an ant: he'll be able to carry something a hundred times his own weight. You, for example, how much do you weigh?"

"I don't know."

"Well, let's say you weigh seventy pounds. If you drink this juice you'll be able to lift . . . seven thousand pounds. You'd be able to lift up this bed with me on it!"

Ilaria lets out her breath.

"You see? The Russians are desperate to have this formula. But Papa doesn't want to give it away because he knows they would use it for bad purposes."

Her small fingers are clenched and white as she clutches the paper.

"For example," I continue, "they'd make all the soldiers in their army drink it as they train to attack the enemy. One Russian alone could pick up ten—what am I saying—a hundred men and hurl them away. Like this!" I twirl the math notebook and toss it in the air.

I pick it up and take the paper from my sister's hands, carefully refold it and slip it into in the notebook. With the same caution, I put the notebook in my backpack.

Ilaria, whose eyes have followed me during this whole process, seems tired out. Her eyes, back to their normal dimensions, have lost their glow.

She says in a whiny voice, "Why doesn't Papa come home?"

"He can't. They're holding him prisoner."

"So why don't we go to rescue him?"

"Because we're still too young. It wouldn't work."

"But you could use the formula! You could hurl all the Russians in the air!"

I gaze up at the ceiling, then back to my sister.

"Even with the formula, we're still too young to take on millions of Russians."

"I'll tell Mamma, she's a grown-up."

"No! Mamma doesn't know anything about it. She thinks Papa is working in Venezuela. If she knew he was a prisoner in Russia, she'd just cry all the time. She'd want to go and free him, but she's too sick. You mustn't say a word about it to her. Swear."

I've managed to frighten her. She swears, crossing her index fingers and kissing them.

"If you tell her Papa is a prisoner in Russia she could drop dead of grief. We two have to protect her."

She assents, lowering her trembling chin.

This time I'm sure she won't say anything.

*   *   *

The front door slams.

The witch doctor.

I leap off the bed and dash into the living room. Mamma's standing between the two armchairs. Her face is ashen.

"Lucio, I was right, you see? But it's worse, much worse than I thought."

Ilaria has joined me, glued to my side. We stare at Mamma. She seems dazed; she might have been crying.

"What do you mean, worse?" I ask.

"Come with me into the bedroom. Illucia, go into Lucio's room and play. Go on, now. Go, I'm telling you!"

Ilaria goes unwillingly, walking backward until she gets to my door. She has her thumb in her mouth.

"Close the door, Lucio."

I close it and follow Mamma into the master bedroom.

She puts her hands on my shoulders and squeezes tight. She stares at me with burning eyes.

"The spell they cast on me is for life. You understand? Till the day I die."

I say nothing. It would be useless to say I don't believe it.

"The legs are the first symptom," she continues, choking up. "The illness will continue until it destroys my whole body. Whoever cast it must have been a very powerful witch or wizard. This *ciarmavermi* says that the witch who casts a spell for life is the only one who can undo it."

"And how much did she charge for this fantastic piece of news?" I burst out, pulling out of her grip.

"Lucio! You don't believe it . . . but she understood right away what kind of spell it was. She's very intuitive, very good at it."

"How much?"

"What do you care? It's none of your business."

"Right. It's none of my business."

I leave the room, put on my jacket and call on my way out, "You're out of your mind to believe that!"

I open the door and I'm out, slamming it behind me.

Chapter 11
Santino

Santino, Papa, and Nonno sat waiting in the car with the windows closed and the motor running. When they arrived at the gate to the Ghost Town, they'd found the square deserted. They were early. Not one of them said a word.

It was totally hushed all around them. The only sound was the hum of the engine. Even the rustle of the wind had stopped. The air outside the car was motionless.

Santino felt restless. The idea of having to plead with Pasquale about his first communion bothered him. It felt stupid, humiliating. At the same time he fervently wished Mamma could have her money back and that the party would make her happy. Without realizing it, he was kicking hard against the front seat.

"Stop that, Santino," his father said.

Santino stopped.

He wasn't thinking about his presents anymore.

There were more serious things to consider: when Mamma found out that the money was gone she would fly into a rage. Forget about kisses. Endless arguments would break out in the house. And Mamma would blame him too. He shifted around and started kicking again.

"Quit it!"

"I'm bored."

"You're bothering us," his father grumbled.

Santino shut up.

To distract himself from his troubled thoughts he began drawing on the fogged-up window pane with his finger. A little house, then alongside it he drew a little man who turned out taller than the house. A giant. He wiped it away with the palm of his hand. Through the cleared portion of the window he could see the gate, and beyond the gate, the long straight road alongside the crumbled houses of the Ghost Town. Way at the end of the road something was moving. Something white.

He rubbed at the window pane again.

A little she-goat, a *capruzza,* that's what it was.

Santino loved baby goats. He loved them so much that at Easter he even refused to eat lamb.

"Papa! Look!"

"What?"

"It's a little *capruzza* over there!" He pointed. "Can I go and pet it?"

"It's better if you stay in the car."

73

Nonno Mico intervened: "We're early. Let him go if he wants to. Here he's nothing but a nuisance. Don't go near the houses, Santù. Stay in the middle of the road, okay?"

"Yes, Nonno."

Santino opened the door and stepped out into the cold. Right away he felt liberated. He passed through the gate and entered the Ghost Town. The goat was far off. She must have found something to nibble on; from where he stood he couldn't tell.

He was careful to walk in the middle of the dusty road, far from the half-destroyed facades with their shattered windows and the branches penetrating them like tentacles. He felt protected by Papa and Nonno, who were surely watching his every step. They couldn't miss him—he was wearing red shoes.

The silence was overpowering. After a quick glance at the houses, he decided to keep his eyes on the goat. There were lots of broken balconies, crumbled staircases, gutted interiors. He was afraid that if he looked too long at those cavernous spaces, he might catch a glimpse of the creeping vines parting and all the people who died in the earthquake coming out. Mangled zombies who would slowly inch their way toward him.

He thought of turning back, the silence was so crushing. But he didn't want to seem like a coward. And there was the little goat, so pretty and white. He wanted to touch her.

He climbed over a semicircular structure surrounded by arches. It was a demolished amphitheater, but to the boy it resembled the immense jaw of a monster. He passed a broad staircase overgrown with grass. Many of the steps were broken, but the stairs went all the way up to an almost intact bell tower.

Despite himself, Santino took it all in with a swift glance: empty windows, iron scaffolding supporting the facades, heaps of rubble, trees stripped bare, arches still undamaged.

He'd seen enough of this dismal place, but by then he was only a few yards away from the goat. He approached her on tiptoe, holding his breath so she wouldn't run away.

"Bianca," he called to her silently.

The animal turned in his direction as if she had heard him. She stared at him with her mild doe eyes, not frightened. They were very close. For a fraction of a second Santino felt himself at one with her. His great delight came out in a huge rush of breath. He could feel the animal's warmth; he and the *capruzza* were the only living beings in the land of the dead. He wanted to put his arms around her. He could smell her gamey skin. He was wild with the urge to get closer and stroke her.

One more step and he could touch her.

The goat sprang up and bounded away with huge leaps.

He thought he must have frightened her. He was so focused on her that it took him a moment to realize that the silence all around him had been shattered by sharp pops, loud as gunshots. Three in a row.

The prolonged echoes filled the air. Meanwhile the *capruzza* was out of sight, leaving him alone in the empty ruins. The shots had come from behind him, from near the gate.

Santino began running in that direction, angry that the noise had made the goat run away. He was still far off when, beyond the grating, he saw a car parked on the square, next to theirs. Two men stood beside it, very still, their backs to him.

He shouted as he ran, his vision blurred, his arms stretched out in front of him. When did the car get there? Where were Papa and Nonno? It wasn't them standing there.

When they heard his shouts, the two men wheeled around.

One of them was *u Taruccatu.*

Santino looked away from Pasquale Loscataglia and toward Papa's car. The shattered windshield, streaked with spatters of blood, leaped out at him like a speeding train. And yet the car didn't move from its place. He stopped at the other side of the gate.

Santino saw nothing more. The earth was shaking under his feet. He blinked his eyes to focus on Papa's car.

Behind the glass, cracked like a burst of sun rays and splotched with red, were two bent-over bodies. Blood was everywhere.

"Papa, Papa, Papa," he yelled, moving forward slowly, struggling against mysterious invisible straps that held him back. The world had turned mute. He couldn't even hear his own voice anymore. He clutched the gate to hold himself up.

As in a horrible nightmare, he saw his grandfather's face, contorted and motionless, his eyes open. He couldn't see Papa's face because he was bent over, as if he were looking for something under the seat. But he was . . . his back was smashed to a pulp like the tomatoes Mamma crushed to make sauce.

Neither one answered his cries. Neither one of them moved.

Dumbfounded, Santino saw Pasquale raise his arm toward him. His dark glasses glinted. His girlish hand, raised up in the air, was gripping something black.

The very instant he recognized the black thing as a pistol, he heard a shot, like a far-off sound heard in a dream.

Santino's red shoes flew off the ground. A fierce shock, a jump, and a sharp pain jolted him out of his stupor. He landed back on his feet.

Instinctively he turned to run. His arm was burning, right below the armpit. He broke into a sprint, the kind of running he knew so well—chest thrust forward, great strides, light and swift—and held his wounded arm stuck to his side. He heard another shot behind him. Instinct told him to move in a zigzag pattern, like in the westerns on TV. This time he didn't worry about going near the houses.

Then, breaking the dull silence behind him, came the sound of swift, heavy footsteps. Someone was chasing him. Someone hated him so much that they wanted to kill him. He didn't turn around; there was no time. He kept on running, the adrenaline released by terror spurring him on.

The main street of the town opened onto a huge empty square. Santino moved toward the side near the houses and leaned his back against a wall to catch his breath, supporting the elbow of his wounded arm with his other hand. The footsteps were coming closer. He turned, but from where he stood he couldn't see who was following him. Whoever it was wouldn't see him either. Too terrified to decide what to do, he moved away from the house and went farther on. Then he paused in front of a half-crumbled front door.

Past the door, a stone staircase. The steps were steep, strewn with rubble, but undamaged. Or so they seemed—a wall cut off his view. Impossible to tell whether those stairs ended in midair.

He stopped, gasping for breath, and leaned his head and shoulders against the wall, still supporting his wounded arm. Were those stairs a trap? Should he keep on running?

Another shot hit him from behind.

This time a searing pain in the back of his leg, below the knee, knocked the wind out of him. His left leg couldn't hold him up anymore. Leaning against the wall, he managed not to fall. The new wound was a flaming blade that twisted his insides. Hopping on his right leg, he slipped into the entryway, then got down on all fours and started up the steps like a puppy. He was dragging his left leg, which put pressure on his right. The pain was atrocious, like nothing he'd ever known. But more adrenaline surged up in him. He advanced, step by step, trying to move fast, but he was slow. There was a second flight of stairs, but the top steps were hidden by the wall. If the stairs ended in midair, he was done for.

He turned for an instant and saw Pasquale entering the house. With a tremendous effort, he got around the corner, faced the second flight and, gathering his strength to climb up the last few steps, dragged himself behind the wall of a room whose floor was still partly intact.

It was very light there. He looked up: no roof. He crawled into a corner and curled his body into a ball, making himself as small as he could. He didn't dare to move for fear the floor would collapse. His whole body was flaming like a torch.

From where he was hidden he couldn't see the staircase. He stayed there, waiting, holding his breath.

He was in a trap. Now it was his turn to die.

Suddenly he didn't care anymore. Papa and Nonno were already dead. Now *u Taruccatu* would kill him too. He heard the heavy footsteps climbing up and thought of his brief life. He felt sorry for Mamma. He felt sorry that now he would never go on those little boats, he couldn't remember what they were called . . . and then his presents, too . . . . He'd never get them. He would die before his first communion. He thought of his friends and how they used to play marbles. He had the best marbles of anyone. He lowered his head, still thinking about the marbles, so he wouldn't see when Pasquale shot him. He noticed his hands, filthy with blood. His own blood. Even his new red shoes were bloodstained, but there the blood didn't show up as much.

More footsteps, coming closer. Pasquale must be on the second flight of stairs.

He squeezed his eyes shut and held his breath, waiting. He concentrated on the colors of his marbles: three were red and opaque, one was turquoise, transparent as the sea of Mondello. There were also two milky-white marbles, but thinking of those upset him—they were like two burnt-out eyes. His favorite was the turquoise. He wished he had it in his pocket right now.

He peed on himself and felt his shorts get all wet. He couldn't do anything about it. If only he could fall asleep.

A booming noise brought him back to his senses. He opened his eyes.

Beneath him something was collapsing. He heard the crash of big chunks of concrete rolling around. A shout. In an instant the air was filled with rubble. It came from below and reached up to where he was huddled. The grainy dust seeped into his wide-open eyes, in his nose, in his open mouth.

From down below came curses. Groans of pain. Swear words. Then another man's voice, one he didn't recognize.

Santino tried to make out the words, but the loud buzzing in his ears didn't let him. He realized he was about to pass out. Now they'd climb up again and get him. Two of them. His whole body was trembling, but oddly enough the pain in his knee and shoulder had become just an irritating throbbing. As if the shoulder and knee didn't belong to him. The two men's voices were fading away—they seemed to come from an astronomical distance, though he knew they were close by. He didn't want those voices. They were Death. He decided to let himself sink into the soft emptiness that was drawing him in. It felt sweet, welcoming, a good hiding place. He let himself go and fainted.

*   *   *

It was the pain that made him come to. Sharp. Fierce as a spike, it was drilling its way through his sleeping body. Then memory returned. Papa's back and Nonno Mico's eyes. No, all that stuff was just a nightmare. He'd been dreaming. You have to forget nightmares right away. He opened his eyes. Why was he curled up on the ground? Where was he?

All around was silence, and in the semidarkness Santino saw, dumbstruck, that the floor ended in an abyss and the side wall stopped halfway up, with a jagged edge. He looked up. The roof was missing. The sky was growing dark.

He remembered.

The chase. Then the shots, the staircase. What had become of Pasquale and the other man? He didn't hear any sound. Did they go away? Why? Something must have happened to the staircase, that was it. It had collapsed. That was why he was still there. They hadn't been able to reach him.

Maybe. Or maybe they were crouching down below, keeping very quiet, waiting for him to come down.

He tried to listen harder to the silence, to see if he could hear them breathing, but he felt very weak. His mouth felt like it was full of sand. He tried to spit, but he had no saliva. He didn't have the strength to move. The pain made him groan softly.

He fainted again.

When at last he opened his eyes, darkness surrounded him. Overhead, the sky was dotted with stars. Under his back, the hard stone floor. He was half stretched out, his legs bent, his head against the wall. All he could think was: it's nighttime.

He was terribly cold. His lips were cracked, they were so dry, and his throat was parched. His leg was throbbing hard, and bit by bit, as he came to, the spike of pain dug deeper into his flesh. But the worst torment was thirst. It muddled his brain.

He stirred slightly and with his good arm touched the wound at the back of his bare leg, below the edge of his shorts. It was all wet. With great effort, he brought his finger soaked with the sticky liquid to his mouth. He licked his own blood and spat to get rid of the plaster dust in his mouth. Again and again and again, very slowly, thinking of nothing. Soon he stopped spitting. He stopped moving altogether—the effort of bringing his hand from below his knee to his lips was too great. His arm fell back down and he passed out again.

Chapter 12

Lucio

I set off to find Monica's bike, seething with rage.

With the money Mamma gave the witch doctor I bet I could have bought a bike as good as hers. But the worst thing is that now Mamma thinks she's going to die. I curse myself for persuading that witch doctor to come to our house. I curse Ilaria, who told her about it.

I unlock the bike and start pedaling furiously. I don't even know where I'm going. Not to Monica's—she can read my mind, and right now I've lost my wits, I'm out of control. It's so bad that if I still had the psychologist I would go see her. With her I could let out all my fears, say dirty words, act crazy, cry. Nothing ever upset her. But I'm too old now; I've got to deal with things on my own. Anyway, I went to Dr. Gaetani by appointment, not whenever I felt like it.

After I pedal aimlessly for an hour, I decide to go back. Mamma's thinking she's near death, and I left her alone with Ilaria, who for all I know is telling her about the Russian spies.

I use my keys to go in, and find Mamma sitting in the armchair with her Illucia in her lap. The little goose's eyes are closed. Mamma's reading her a fairy tale. She doesn't stop even when I come near.

I crouch down near them and listen. After a moment Ilaria opens her eyes and gives me a sign to go away. Mamma keeps reading in a low voice, so I go to my room.

I stretch out on the bed without taking off my shoes. I don't know why I'm so depressed.

Under my bed is the small box where I keep my gear for the Optimist. I check it often in winter to make sure everything is in place: duct tape, screwdriver, pocket knife, hook, sandpaper, and a whole lot of other stuff.

I take it out, open it carefully, and pick up the knife. It's an Indian knife I saw in a store window downtown. Even though it's not a switchblade, it opens and closes easily. The handle is wood with little brass studs. Once it's out, the thin blade looks long and sharp. It commands respect. The person who sold it to me hesitated because of my age. I answered by showing my Nautical Club card and explaining that it was part of my equipment. I used the money that was left over after the shopping.

I open it and stroke the sharp edge with my fingertip, then close it and put it back in the box. I feel around in the bottom for my letters to the Hunter. This winter I wrote him only five. They'll have to wait for summer. I put the box back in its place and lie down on the bed. I arrange the pillow under my head. I stare at the ceiling. I fall asleep.

I wake up forty-five minutes later. In the dream I was chased by a torrent of lava. I ran at breathtaking speed across a desolate landscape, doing slaloms between bare skeletal trees.

I don't hear any sounds coming from the living room. I get up and open the door quietly.

Mamma is alone, sewing in the armchair. She's wearing her glasses; she's embroidering a sheet, the same one she's been working on for a week. She hasn't heard me, so I gaze at her for a long moment.

It's strange—when you look at a familiar person who doesn't know they're being observed, it's like seeing a stranger.

Bent over her sewing, Mamma strikes me as an old peasant woman. Her face isn't wrinkled, but it's a bit puffy; her eyes are sunken. Her movements are precise, but you can see she doesn't care about what she's doing. She's fat—it's not just her elephant legs; her body is thick and heavy too.

I draw near and she looks up. "Shh . . . Ilaria's asleep in the big bed."

"First, I apologize," I say under my breath.

She looks at me in silence and sighs. "You're a good son."

"Ma, I have an idea. Listen." I move closer. Mamma lets the sheet fall and opens her arms. I sit on the floor and put my head on her big lap.

She puts her hand on my hair and leaves it there, not moving.

For a while we stay like that, silent, breathing softly.

Finally I raise my head to face her.

"Don't you want to hear my idea?"

"Of course, Lucio."

"Okay, then. Do you know who's the best and most powerful of all the witches in the world?"

"No. Do you?"

"It's the Madonna! She can perform whatever miracles she wants to. And the Madonna of Montenero is truly strong. She saved a bunch of sailors from hurricanes. She could certainly undo that spell that could kill you."

Mamma gazes at me open-mouthed.

I go on: "My idea is that I should go to the sanctuary and promise her an ex voto, which means I'll give her a picture with . . . with . . . a picture that shows your sickness. But only after you're better."

"Lucio, my boy, maybe you're right." Mamma strokes my face.

I avoid her hand. "That's it! That's what I'll do. I'll make a vow that if you're cured I won't sail on the Optimist anymore."

"I don't want that. It's not necessary. But I do like the idea of your going to the sanctuary to pray for me. The Madonna will listen to my children's prayers, because they're two angels."

"Okay," I say, even though I'm planning to go to the sanctuary alone, pedaling hard all the way up the hill on Monica's bike, so I can coast all the way back down. Otherwise we'd have to take the bus and it would be a drag. But this isn't the moment to discuss it.

Chapter 13

Santino

When Santino opened his eyes, it seemed he'd been transported inside a cloud. Glaring light, blurry outlines, and a strange pungent smell.

He blinked. It wasn't a cloud in the sky. He was in a room where everything was pure white—ceiling, walls, chairs—so white that it was hard to distinguish one thing from another. Too much light. It blinded him.

He wasn't cold anymore. He was wrapped in softness. No pain.

The place was unfamiliar. The smell of the air was unfamiliar too. He tried to move but he was numb. He wanted to lift his head to see better where he was, but he couldn't manage it.

A dark shadow fell between him and the too bright light. An undulating shape moving toward him. He couldn't get it into focus. It moved closer, and only when it was almost just above him did he realize it was a human face.

It looked like Mamma. But it was also different. The woman towered above him, so close he could feel her breath. A face distorted by shock. Something black covered her hair. It was strange to see Mamma dressed like that: she hated black. She looked like a crow. That made him want to laugh, but the laugh made no sound. He tried harder, but the laugh just wouldn't come out.

I'm in Paradise, he thought. He closed his eyes and opened them again. Crow-Mamma had moved off and was calling someone.

"He's waking up," he heard her shout hoarsely. "Hurry up!"

A second shape approached. Santino squinted again: it was a different woman, with a white cap and round face, who bent over him. Now he had two faces above him, one light, one dark.

"He's awake," White-Cap agreed. "How do you feel, sweetheart? Are you able to speak?"

Instead of answering, he shifted his glance toward the face of the woman in black. Crow-Mamma was crying.

Santino made a grimace. A piercing pain, a sharp fragment of hell rose from deep inside him, invading and spreading through his body. He'd forgotten that pain, but now, as it spread, he recognized it. He'd felt it before, he didn't know when.

White-Cap was bustling around him. He felt a pinprick. Gradually the pain subsided, freeing his body so he could relax. He noticed lots of wires attached to his skin: blue and yellow tubes. He was exhausted.

Paradise is weird, thought Santino, closing his eyes on all that weirdness.

In an instant he was fast asleep again.

*   *   *

When he awoke his vision was clearer. He explored with his eyes, barely moving his head, which still felt as heavy as a ripe watermelon.

He was in a room. All white but full of strange machines. A woman dressed in white was sitting in a corner, dozing. She had a round face and a white cap that seemed to sparkle in the electric light. Santino thought he'd seen her before, in a dream.

As if she sensed the boy's glance, the woman opened her eyes, got up, and came over to the bed. "Santino, can you hear me?" she asked softly.

Santino didn't have the strength to answer, but he gave a tiny nod of his head.

"I'm Rosa, the nurse. You were hurt and you had an operation. Now you're in the recovery room, but you're already doing better. Do you understand?"

Another minuscule nod, yes.

Rosa took his slender wrist between two fingers, then

pulled down his lower lids and looked into his eyes. She checked the colored tubes and the bags hanging from metal rods.

"Mamma," Santino mumbled.

"She'll be here in a minute. First I have to call the doctor who's been taking care of you these last few days."

"Mamma," Santino repeated. His voice was panicky.

The nurse reassured him: "She's waiting right outside. You'll see her in just a minute."

"Mamma, Mamma, Mamma."

"Don't get upset. Here's the doctor."

A man in a smock and cap had entered. The two were muttering something to each other. Santino closed his eyes.

Someone was patting his body here and there, but he kept his eyes closed tight to shut out that intrusive touch. A man's voice: "So here you are, Santino. You had a narrow escape, you know? What you went through would have killed a grown-up. But not you! You have a strong constitution."

Santino didn't answer.

"Take him out of the induced coma. Disinfect his wounds while he's still under some sedation and then transfer him to ward three," the man's voice instructed.

"He wants to see his mother."

"After he's transferred."

"Mamma!" shrieked Santino. That is, he thought he screeched, but in fact his voice was thin as a hair.

"Soon. Your Mamma is a sensitive person. We don't want to scare her, do we?"

He heard footsteps leaving the room. The click of the door.

"Don't be afraid of the doctor." It was the nurse, who was still in the room. "Or of me either. I'll be very careful. You won't feel a thing."

Santino was overcome by sleep even before the nurse began. He slipped slowly into a cocoon of silence and didn't feel anything she was doing to his body.

* * *

He was dreaming. He was at home, in the kitchen. Nonno and Nonna were there, Papa, Mamma, and also Uncle Turi, Mamma's brother. Instead of talking as usual, they were all whispering and their whispers gathered into a hum, like ghosts plotting something. He asked what they were doing, but no one answered. From the mantelpiece the weasel jumped onto the table, scattering plates and glasses. But even then the disturbing whispers didn't stop. He woke up, but the murmur was still in his ears. He opened his eyes.

The woman in black who looked like his mother was standing a few feet from the bed. She had her back to her brother. Uncle Turi, burly, scowling, and dressed in black, was muttering something to her. Santino couldn't understand the words. But Mamma—he was almost certain it was her—tightened her lips as if disapproving of what the man was murmuring, without ever turning to face him.

"Mamma," Santino mumbled.

The woman rushed to him. Was it Mamma?

"Santù, Santù." She burst into tears.

"Assunta, don't do that, it'll upset him." Uncle Turi came over and took her by the shoulders, pulling her back. He gripped her with his arms. "Let's call the nurse."

So he was in a hospital. Now he remembered. But the room was different from the one before. There was a television, everything looked more cheerful, and that stinging smell was gone.

"What happened?" asked Santino in a thick voice, almost too garbled to make out.

"My baby, it's a miracle that you're alive! A miracle!" Assunta shook off her brother's grip and returned to the bedside. "You're safe, sweetheart!" She stroked his face.

Santino wanted to smile. He also wanted to ask her why she was dressed in black, but it took too much effort to move his tongue.

The door opened and the nurse came in. "Be careful, don't tire him. He's only been out of the induced coma for two hours."

"Is he out of danger?" asked Assunta.

"I'd say definitely yes. Later we'll have him eat something." The woman with the cap glanced at the door.

"They're waiting out there. They'll want to interrogate him today, but don't worry. I'll say it's not possible and the doctor will confirm that. They'll come back tomorrow."

"So soon?" Assunta protested.

"They're in a hurry, you understand . . . ."

"Are the police still in the hall?" asked Uncle Turi.

Santino was astonished. The police? Uncle Turi always called them pigs and steered clear of them.

"Certainly. They'll stay there as long as the child is in this room. They take turns. Twenty-four seven. You can rest easy."

Uncle Turi frowned. "So, Assunta, I'll leave you two alone. And you, *picciriddu*, concentrate on getting well."

His uncle bent over to give him a kiss. His mouth smelled of smoke. He moved toward the door with heavy steps. "I'm warning you," he said, turning to his sister before he left. "Remember what I told you."

Assunta shot him a sullen glance.

"I'm Teresa," the nurse told Santino. "Now I'm going to wash you. Then the doctor will see you, and then you can eat. Signora, it would be best if you went out for a moment."

Mamma drew close to Santino and kissed him. "I'll be right there in the hall, don't be scared."

But Santino was indeed scared, so scared that he got very upset. "No, don't go away," he wailed. "Stay here!"

"You can stay if you like. Move over there, where you won't be in the way and your son can see you."

Teresa brought over a cart with a basin, sponge, soap, and towels. It was funny to be washed lying down, like an infant. Santino fixed his eyes on his mother's face. He spluttered when the nurse passed the wet, soapy sponge over his face. Then she gently rubbed his neck, his hands, and so on, avoiding his bandaged leg and arm.

Santino didn't pay attention to what she was doing; he preferred to keep looking at Mamma. She looked peculiar: besides the black kerchief on her head and her black clothes, she seemed twenty years older. Those wrinkles—she'd never had them before. Also, her mouth was different. Thinner, withered. And her eyes were sunken in her face, as if some nasty person had shoved them in.

The soapy sponge went over his genitals and Santino opened his eyes wide. Then as the wet cloth moved down his good leg, he picked up his train of thought.

Maybe he'd slept for twenty years, like in "Sleeping Beauty," and meanwhile everyone had grown old.

"Now I need you to turn on your side. Let me know if I'm hurting you," Teresa told him.

Santino turned onto his side but managed to keep his eyes fixed on Assunta, who returned his mute gaze, her lips drawn into a pained smile.

Teresa, meanwhile, kept talking to him in a gentle voice: "Soon you'll be all better, you know? Your surgeon is the best one in the city. Your leg will be like new. It's a good thing your knee wasn't hit. As for your arm . . . you're lucky, no serious fractures. It'll be as good as new before you know it. There, one more minute and I'm done."

Santino, who didn't feel quite so lucky, wanted to ask how come he had so many injuries, but he couldn't summon the strength to speak. Not while that woman was fussing over his body. Could he possibly have slept so long? And yet Uncle Turi hadn't changed. He hadn't grown old. It was all so strange. He didn't remember how he had ended up in the hospital.

"There, all done." Teresa resettled him on his back. "You were great, braver than a grown man. Now the doctor will see you and then you can have something to eat." She turned to Assunta. "Don't wear him out. Don't talk to him too much for now."

Santino lowered his eyelids. He'd never in his life felt so exhausted, not even when he ran behind Papa's car. He heard the door close and a hand took hold of his.

"My sweet baby."

Even Mamma's voice had changed. It didn't use to be so hoarse. Assunta had dragged the armchair next to the bed.

"Ma, how old am I now?" asked Santino in a wisp of a voice, barely opening his eyes.

"You're six years and eleven months, my darling. Almost seven." She smiled a weak, sad smile.

"So I didn't sleep so long."

"You were in a deep sleep for three weeks. The doctors thought that would be best, after the operation."

"What happened to me?"

Mamma hesitated. "Later," she said in a low voice. "Later, when you're feeling better. Now you mustn't tire yourself out."

"I remember . . . a white *capruzza*. Where did she go?"

"Shh."

"Did I see her in a dream?"

"I think so."

"And I saw a broken window. It was a horrible nightmare. Our car was spattered with blood and I was so scared."

"My baby, my precious, don't think about it now."

"Why do you look so old?"

"I was so afraid of losing you. Fear makes people look older."

"Oh, so that's why. And Papa? Where is he?"

Santino knew right away that there was something wrong about his question. His mother's whole face crumpled up, and he too felt a shiver when he uttered the word "Papa." The image of a big iron gate flashed before him. That gate was terrifying.

Assunta looked at him anxiously but didn't answer.

Someone was knocking on the door. It was the doctor. Santino kicked with his good leg.

The doctor approached. "Are you afraid of me?"

Silence.

"I'm not going to hurt you. I'm the surgeon who operated on you and I want to see if I did a good job. Then I'll know how soon you'll get better."

But Santino was still scared.

"What are you afraid of?"

"I don't know."

The doctor smiled and came even closer to the bed. Santino stiffened. Assunta, in the meantime, had returned to her place near the window.

"I know all about your arm and leg. I know how they're put together. You have lots of important tiny bones. If you want to see, I can show you the X-rays. That way you can know how you're put together too."

Santino gave a little smile.

"You're the hero of the day, you know that? Everyone's talking about you."

Santino, still a bit nervous, was checking out the doctor's movements; he was examining his wounded limbs as he spoke.

"Do you remember what happened?" the big man asked abruptly.

"A *capruzza*."

"And then?"

"I had an awful nightmare."

"Don't think about that now. For now you should think only about getting better. We'll have you up on your feet very soon, kiddo. You'll be playing ball as well as before. Even better than before! Do you watch the soccer games on TV? I never miss a single one."

"You're not Sicilian?" Santino asked.

The man smiled. "Yes, I am, but I lived in Turin starting when I was younger than you. I've only been in Palermo for two years. That's why I don't have the same accent as you. You're a smart boy, you noticed right away."

While he was talking he had listened to Santino's heart, tapped his good leg and arm, and done other things the boy couldn't keep track of. When the examination was over the surgeon spoke under his breath to Mamma, patted her warmly on the shoulder, and left the room.

A few minutes later came another knock on the door. "Lunch is here!" a voice rang out. A pretty young woman entered the room pushing a cart. She too was wearing a cap and a white smock. She smiled. "I'm Paola."

She began slowly cranking up the back of the bed with a lever, then arranged the cart, turning the table until it was in front of Santino's chest. She uncovered the plates. "Mashed potatoes, chicken breast, baked apple. Mmm, does that sound good?"

Santino nodded, staring at her. He'd never seen such a beautiful creature. Blue eyes, freckles. And a smile so warm that it felt like a big hug.

"A perfect ten," he whispered.

Paola didn't hear him.

"I can feed you—would you like that?"

Chapter 14

Lucio

It's been three months since Ilaria and I went to make the vow at the sanctuary of Montenero, but Mamma's legs still look like tree trunks. On the other hand, Monica's ankle healed much too fast. I gave her back her bike.

Since she's gone back to her dance classes we don't see each other as much. I figured out how many hours we've spent together. Not many, compared to before.

My life is monotonous: school, homework, Ilaria, TV news, shopping, then Ilaria again. The only changes are that I haven't gone back to Carmelo's fish stand at the market, to avoid the *ciarmavermi*, and my sister's cheeks have lost their fiery color because the cold weather here in Livorno is over.

My birthday, April 7th, passed at school without anything special. None of the kids wished me happy birthday. How could they? No one knew about it. At home, Mamma gave me a hug and two shirts, and Ilaria gave me a drawing and ordered me to hang it up on the wall of my room.

Luckily, it won't be long now before training at the nautical club starts up again. All these years Mamma's let me go only in summer, after school is out. During the long winter break I train on my own.

What I do is: on the bus, or stretched out on my bed, or walking alongside Ilaria, I imagine myself tacking, jibing, and steering around buoys. I visualize it all. I imagine having to struggle against a west wind, and figure out the maneuvers I'd have to make.

Then there's the little box under the bed. Every now and then I open it and take out the things that are stored there. I hold them up, I clean them. I add a letter.

But now, school will be over in a week and I've stopped my imaginary nautical training: final exams are coming. One of Mamma's conditions for my racing with the Optimist is that I have to do well in school.

This year I can relax. I should get good grades.

* * *

Today I take the little goose on the bus to a beach that's farther away. Between the big rocks, there's a stretch of rough, flat stones that leads to the sea. There are some natural holes that are perfectly round, the size of a pot, and full of water.

As soon as Ilaria reaches that stretch with the round holes, she crouches down, throws stones in and starts stirring them with a small stick. She's making dinner. Hours go by. She's quiet and I can go for a swim.

I've barely set out when I see her leap up and run toward the stairs leading from the street down to the beach. I turn and see Monica and Ricky coming down.

"Did you come by bike?" I ask.

"Yes, Ricky rode in the basket."

She undresses in a flash, down to her bathing suit. Her skin is barely tan, not dark like mine.

"I'm going to take a swim. You want to come?" I ask.

"And your sister?"

"She can stay with Ricky."

Monica looks at Ilaria doubtfully, then at me.

"Trust me. I'll keep an eye on them."

"Okay. Go get undressed, I'll wait for you."

"I'm already undressed," I point out.

"You go swimming in your shorts and T-shirt?"

"I'm allergic to the sun, okay?"

We go in the water and after a few strokes we stop and turn toward the rocks to check on Ilaria and Ricky, who are playing together. I do a backflip underwater. She does one too, and I see she's much better than I am.

I go under again. As soon as I come back up she imitates me, disappearing in turn. I'm not as flexible and precise. She looks like an athlete. It must be because of the dancing.

"Tomorrow I'm going to the Tirreno Baths with Stella and Oriana," Monica says, resurfacing. "You want to come?"

I have no idea who Stella and Oriana are, but I know the Tirreno Baths are where the Aqua-Park is. It has a huge swimming pool with a great water slide.

"I start training tomorrow. We're going to the Tirreno Baths for Ilaria's birthday, July 13th. That's Mamma's birthday present to her."

"I won't be here on the thirteenth."

"Where are you going?"

"We're going on vacation in three days. To Sardinia."

I feel awful. "In three days?"

"Yes. We're dying of the heat here. It's not good for Duccio."

"So we'll see each other at the end of the summer."

My face has become unreadable. Or close to it, I hope.

Ricky's running toward the water. Ilaria jumps up to follow him.

Without another word, with a few swift strokes, we head toward shore to meet them.

*   *   *

I didn't sleep last night. But now I'm at the sailing club for the first training session of the season. I have my box of equipment with me.

I say hi to everyone and look around for my boat. Enrico, the coach, points it out, clapping me on the shoulder.

I go over to the Optimist, which is covered with a tarp. I know it's still disassembled. It's been there all winter, waiting for me.

There are a million things to take care of, more urgent than talking to the other guys. I've already put on my shorts and T-shirt.

First of all, I need to fit out the boat, which needs to be done very carefully. I put up the mast, open the sail and stretch it, make sure the flotation devices are full, and a bunch of other things.

Once it's all finished, I gaze out over the surface of the sea to check the wind and the current. But the coach is already telling us what conditions we'll find.

We carry the boats to the water—this is hard, and we're impatient.

Once I'm on the water, finally alone in my small boat, I move away from the dock. Then I have to wait for the others. Never go out into the open sea till everyone has left port: that's the rule.

When we're all there and the sails fill the sky, I position myself sideways so my bottom is outside of the boat, almost touching the water. I pull the halyard like the accelerator of a motorbike and the boat takes off fast over the waves.

With the wind lashing at my face, the boat skimming along, the waves crashing at me, my real life begins.

My body merges with the boat: we're one unique thing. The waves are huge today, and when the boat comes down in a controlled glide and reaches the bottom, there's an instant, a single instant, before it rises again, when I'm closed in between two mountains of water, the horizon hidden by liquid walls, and I feel totally alive. The sky is my own. The sea is my own. I am my own!

This is the moment I when I hurl my letters to the Hunter overboard. I've been holding them tight between my teeth, all ready, since I reached the open sea. I grab them with one hand and toss them away.

The envelopes fly off like white birds riding on the wind. I don't see them land on the water because a wave, like a great liquid hand, has already caught me, to carry me back up. It's the moment when all the boredom of the winter flows out of my body, freeing it from all the dusty remains. I feel cleared out, clean.

The order to return to shore, at the end of the training session, always comes too soon. When I'm back in the locker room, changing behind my door, the other boys fool around and chatter joyfully, but I'm silent. I want to preserve inside me that azure groove of the wave that carries my letters far away.

Chapter 15
Santino

S antino woke from his nightmare in a sweat and trembling. Darkness was all around him. He was seized by panic and threw off the covers.

He had dreamed of the windshield spattered with blood and his father's back reduced to raw meat. His grandfather, behind the broken window, was staring at him. Instead of eyes he had two milky white marbles. And *u Taruccatu* was standing there too. Dark glasses, quivering mustache, a pistol in his hand. And another man, barely a shadow, but huge.

He gasped for breath again and again, but the monstrous scene, drenched in the stench of death, didn't leave him. He was fleeing. He didn't realize that all the while his good leg was kicking between the sheets.

He shut his eyes, hoping that the dark would erase the awful vision, but the scene of horror was still there, etched in fire beneath his eyelids. It had all the details and consistency of reality. It couldn't be true, but it was.

Then came the clear vision of the ruins. And with that, his memories resurfaced. He and Papa and Nonno had gone to the Ghost Town. They had to give back the money. They were waiting in the car. Then he'd seen the little white goat.

The *capruzza* darted away.

The animal's leap, the shots. Utterly incredible.

"Papi! Papi!" he screamed in the dark. "Papi papi papi . . . ."

The light went on and Mamma was beside him.

"Easy, easy, you'll make yourself sick . . . ." She bent over him. She tried to put the covers back on him, but he struggled and wouldn't let her.

"Where's Papa?"

Assunta let go of the covers and sat down gingerly on the bed. Santino couldn't make her out clearly; he couldn't see her crying.

"Your papa is in heaven," she said softly. Santino didn't hear her. She said it again, louder.

"In heaven? What is he doing there?"

"He's fine, he's watching over us, you and me."

"And Nonno?"

"He's keeping him company."

Santino was silent. It was hard to breathe.

Mamma bent over him again to kiss his face. "Still, be still."

He felt the wet taste of salt on his own lips. "They were shot," he said with a sob.

"My darling . . . ."

"They killed Papa too."

"So you remember?" Assunta asked.

"I was right in the middle of the shooting." Santino stared at her with a fierce intensity.

So his memory was back.

"Don't think about it now," she murmured, giving him wet kisses on his face, on his sweaty neck, on his hands. "Does anything hurt? Should I call the nurse? She'll make it go away. Maybe that cute one's on duty, the one you like. I saw how you looked at her yesterday."

Santino barely moved his head to say no. "Stay here," he whispered.

"Alfonso is in heaven and he can hear us," she repeated. "Nonno Mico is with him."

The boy wiggled his good leg, bent his knee and raised it, then bounced it again under the sheet, like someone trying to run using only one side of his body. He was mumbling something, and looked as though he might be delirious.

Assunta rang the bell and the nurse came in. It wasn't the cute one.

In his awful agitation, Santino kept banging his leg and arm. He couldn't even see anymore.

* * *

When he awoke, Mamma wasn't in the room. Someone had put the covers back on him.

The young nurse was with him. Paola. She was adjusting the drip on the tube.

"Ah, so you're awake," she said when she saw his eyes were open. "How do you feel? Any better?"

"Yes," Santino answered. "A tiny, tiny bit better."

"That's how it starts, little by little, until you're completely better." She bent over and smiled. "Can I give you a little kiss?"

For an instant she put her lips on the boy's damp cheek.

"You're so pretty." Santino blew a kiss into the air with his dry lips.

"You really think I'm pretty?"

"A number ten."

"How do you like this *picciriddu* . . . ."

"Do it again."

"You want another kiss?" Her motherly tenderness made him feel good. "Soon I'll bring your breakfast." She was about to leave when she remembered something and turned back.

"I was the one who undressed you before the operation. I had to take this off too . . . ." She opened the drawer of the night table, poked around for a moment, and took out a small object. "Now you can put it back on. I'll help you. I've never seen a trinacria like this. It's really . . . ."

Santino started yelling over her words. "No no no no! Throw it away!"

The nurse stepped back and instinctively stuck the charm in her shirt pocket so the boy wouldn't see it. "Okay. Fine. Calm down."

"Throw it away! Throw it away!"

"Yes, yes, I'll throw it away, but please be calm."

She seemed frightened. She went back toward the bed and smiled. "I don't want to scare you." She stroked his cheek. Her hand was soft and warm.

Watching her, Santino gradually calmed down.

There came a knock on the door.

Uncle Turi came in and said hello. From the look on his face, he wasn't pleased to find the nurse in the room.

Paola lingered a moment to smooth Santino's sheets and put back the blanket that had fallen again, then she left, promising to return with his breakfast.

His uncle approached the bed and greeted his nephew, asked how he was, then began silently circling the room. He was studying the walls. He moved a picture aside to see what was behind it. He looked for a long time at the TV, which was off. He touched the lamp. He inspected the electrical outlets. He even bent down to look under the bed.

"Where's Mamma?" Santino asked.

"She's at the hospital café getting coffee." Uncle Turi came close. "She was awfully tired. She'll be back in a little while. She told me that . . . ." He bent down further and brushed Santino's ear with his lips. "That last night you remembered something."

"Papa went to heaven," Santino said in a toneless voice. "And Nonno Mico went to keep him company."

Uncle Turi nodded gravely. "Yes, that's right. But you were saved, which is a miracle for us."

Santino noticed that Uncle Turi resembled a hippopotamus. Because of the skin drooping from his chin and also because he was so fat. It was the first time that had occurred to him. He was so close that he could smell his bitter odor. It wasn't anything like Mamma's smell, and yet they were brother and sister.

"What happened? Who was there?"

At the urgent whisper aimed right into his ear, the boy began wriggling around in bed as he had at night, kicking with his good leg.

It was hard to bring out the words. "It wasn't a horrible nightmare. It was all true."

"So you know who was there."

He didn't answer. It bothered him to feel his uncle's lips stuck to his ear like a leech. He really stank.

Turi cleared his throat. "Very soon, maybe even today, the cops will be coming to see you. They'll ask a ton of questions. You won't say a word. Tell them you can't remember anything."

"Why?"

"Because we don't talk to cops. Ever."

Santino nodded uncertainly.

"It's who we are. *Cosa nostra*,"* his uncle went on, still whispering in his ear with an insidious calm. "It's our own business. You wouldn't want to be a rat, would you? Didn't your father teach you any self-respect? If you talk to those filthy cops you'll betray us all, you understand?"

The boy covered his eyes.

"But first there'll be people coming who aren't cops who'll ask you about your parents, how old you are, that kind of thing. You can answer them if you really want to. But it's better if you play dumb. That way you won't make any mistakes."

The door opened and Mamma entered.

Uncle Turi quickly straightened up and moved off from the bed. Santino was relieved.

Assunta rushed to her son. "You're up, my darling." Then she turned toward her brother and asked suspiciously, "What were you talking about?"

"Nothing," Turi replied. "I asked him how he was feeling and told him that he'd be going home soon. I promised to bring him a coloring book with crayons. Right, Santù?"

She studied her brother warily for an instant. Then she looked back at her son, one eyebrow raised in a question.

Santino didn't know if he should lie for his uncle. He'd rather say nothing. His head was still all mixed up.

---

* *Cosa Nostra*: "Our thing," in Italian. It is another term for the Mafia.

"They're coming to see him soon, first the doctor, then a psychiatrist and a psychologist," said Assunta. "They'll make us leave. Or maybe I can stay, I don't know."

"Fine, I know when I'm not wanted." Uncle Turi shot a hostile look at his sister, and a quick warning glance, like a lightning flash, at Santino. He walked to the door. On his way out he crossed paths with a doctor who was coming in.

*   *   *

"Mamma. I remember everything now," whispered Santino as soon as the doctor had gone. The doctor—not the surgeon with the mustache from the day before—was satisfied with his physical condition. He repeated what everyone said: it was a miracle that he was alive.

The boy wanted to talk and find out more about what had happened to him.

"I heard the shots, you know, and I hid," he confided weakly to his mother, barely holding the hand gripping his. "But I don't know how I got here."

"That was another miracle." Assunta spoke gently and softly. "The staircase collapsed after you climbed up."

"I heard it falling down."

"Whoever was following you must have fallen."

"There were two of them."

"Luckily the police got a phone call, otherwise you would have bled to death."

"Who called them?"

"No one knows. It was an anonymous call. They think it might have been a thief who snuck into one of the houses in the Ghost Town to steal something. The police got there at dawn. They found the car with . . . with Papa and Nonno."

She paused a moment to look at her son, who was silent. Seeing that he was still calm, she went on.

"When they found the trail of blood you left on the road between the ruins, they followed it. That's how they got to the house where you were hiding. The steps were gone and the trail of blood ended there, on the rubble. They thought there might be someone wounded up there, so they called the firemen, who came with their ladder. They climbed up and found you. You were still breathing. They took you away in an ambulance and then here in a helicopter."

"A helicopter!" Santino exclaimed, astonished. "Too bad I was sleeping."

"Yes, it's too bad."

"I was in a helicopter," he repeated, excited.

"When you're all better we'll take a plane ride together, you and me."

"Really? Will we go above the clouds and see Papa and Nonno?"

"Yes, above the clouds."

Santino realized Mamma was thinking of something else.

"What did Uncle Turi say to you," Assunta asked.

"That I mustn't speak to the cops."

"I thought so." Assunta looked around, then instructed him in a loud voice: "You have to tell them everything. You . . . tell EVERYTHING you remember."

Mamma seemed to be trembling as she stressed that *everything*. He wanted to talk more about the helicopter. This conversation was making him all confused. He was getting tired. What did they really expect of him? He didn't want to be a rat. And why did his uncle look around the room in that strange way? What was he looking for? And why did Mamma suddenly start talking in such a loud voice?

It was all too complicated.

"Mamma, can Paola come with us in the helicopter too?"

"Ah, so you have a crush on her? Is she your *zita*?* She's very pretty."

"Yes, my *zita*." Santino closed his eyes and fell fast asleep.

---

* *Zita*: fiancée, girlfriend, in Sicilian dialect.

Chapter 16
Lucio

Ilaria is dressed in pink again. Summer pink: jeans, T-shirt, and baseball cap. Underneath she already has on her bathing suit, also pink. In these clothes she just got as a birthday gift, the little piglet jumps around like she's possessed: she's convinced she's adorable.

"Ma, why don't you come too? Let's take a taxi."

This isn't an unselfish suggestion: if Mamma comes with us she'll take care of Ilaria and I can do whatever I want. I've never gone to the Tirreno baths. There are private beaches with cabanas and everything, maybe the fanciest in Livorno.

Mamma looks at me, surprised.

"Just this one time."

She grabs Ilaria by the arm, takes out her barrettes, and slowly combs her hair.

"Yes, Mamma, you come too!" Ilaria cries.

She stops combing and gives one of her sighs. "What would I do at the Baths? I can't put on a bathing suit, I'm

117

not a good swimmer, I'd be hot and that's it. All that *picciuli* thrown away." Another sigh. "You two go and enjoy the day. You can eat there. I'll stay home where it's cool and for once I won't cook. Here, Lucio, here's some money."

*   *   *

We walk there: the Tirreno Baths are near the Mascagni terrace. At the entrance I hand over the money and they give us a key for a private changing room. For Ilaria the fun has already started: she pretends the cabana is a little cottage. I help her get undressed. I keep on my tank top and swimming trunks. I finally drag her away by force from the suffocating little hole that smells of wood, sweat, and sunscreen.

The pool is immense. Ilaria stops short at the sight of it. She says the water slide is too high. It scares her.

I say we'll go together. With me she doesn't have to be afraid of anything.

We line up with the other kids to go up the metal steps. When it's our turn, we sit down with her in front and me holding her tight around the waist.

"Ready?"

"No, wait!"

"Look at that whole line behind us. Ready?"

"Ye . . . es."

I give her a push. Sliding down, we both scream until we tumble into the water. I keep hold of her because the pool is deep. She gasps, clinging to my neck.

"Again!" she shrieks.

We go on the slide together thirteen times—I count them. Then I've had it. "I'm hungry," I say. "Are you?"

"Yes, a little. But first let's go one more . . . ."

"Listen, first we're going to the cottage to change. Today you can order whatever you want. It's your birthday!"

We finally get to the restaurant. Lots of people are already at the tables. I see big pizzas on the plates. Perfect. We move toward a free table and . . . .

"Ilaria! Ilaria!" a child's voice calls. From a table where a couple is seated, a little girl is waving wildly at my sister.

Ilaria runs over. It's Maria, one of her friends from pre-school. Her parents introduce themselves: Anna Rosa and Stefano. They order pizzas for us. I explain that Ilaria is five years old today.

"Ilaria's birthday?" Anna Rosa says. "Where are Mamma and Papa?" She looks around, surprised.

I explain very briefly the way things are.

Ilaria sits next to Maria. The two of them do nothing but giggle and whisper nonsense into each other's ears. Stefano says it's too bad they've got to go home at three o'clock. He and Anna Rosa huddle together, making plans.

Anna Rosa looks up: "We have to go soon. Would you like to come to our house? We live a few kilometers from

Livorno. So Ilaria and Maria could be together for a little longer."

Ilaria and Maria bang their spoons on the table making a racket: "Yes yes yes yes yes!"

"We still have time for an ice cream," says Anna Rosa. "But it would be good to let your mother know."

I put my hand in the shorts pocket to get my cell phone. It's not there. I must have left it in my room. "It doesn't matter," I say. "Mamma doesn't expect us yet—she said we could stay out all day."

We go back to our cabanas and meet again two minutes later at the gate. We get in the car, the parents up front and the three of us in the back.

They live in a small private house with a garden. While Maria shows my sister all the toys in her room, Stefano offers me a bunch of old Snoopy comics. "Pardon me if I don't keep you company, but I have to wait in my office for a phone call from the United States. Business. Feel free to go into the garden, there's a hammock," he tells me. "Don't worry about Ilaria."

Stretched out in the hammock, rocking gently, I enjoy the old comic books. They're funny. I stay there reading until they call me for tea. There's also a really nice cake—Anna Rosa just made it. She wrote "Ilaria" on top with icing. After we eat the cake it's time to go, but the two friends shriek in protest. Stefano offers to drive us home. Maria wants to come along, to stay a little longer with Ilaria.

They drop us a few feet from our door. We get out, but Ilaria won't move until the car is out of sight.

"It's better not to tell Mamma that we left the baths so early," I warn her.

"Why?"

I explain with a just a touch of malice: "She might be hurt that you preferred your friend to the Aqua Park—that was her birthday gift."

She gives a blank stare. "Why?"

"Oh, let it go."

I open the outside door with my key.

Chapter 17
Santino

A man in a white doctor's coat and cap entered the room that was guarded by the police. He had a thin face, a salt-and-pepper mustache, and a thick head of gray hair.

Santino started trembling. He kicked with his leg as if to run away. His eyes filled with terror.

"I'm Guglielmo Gigli, the children's neuropsychiatrist," said the imposing man as he went to shake Assunta's hand. "Are you the mother?"

"Yes."

"Stay, by all means. This will be a very brief first interview. I don't want to tire him out, but I need to evaluate as early as possible his ability to testify." He went toward the bed.

"Hi, Santino, can you hear me?"

The boy nodded, terrified.

"Are you afraid of me?"

Again he nodded.

"What are you afraid of?"

Santino pointed to him with a vague gesture.

"My height?"

He shook his head.

"My eyes?"

Another no with his head. The boy put his finger on his mouth.

"This?" said the man, running a finger over his mustache.

A tiny nod, yes.

"My mustache. Why does my mustache scare you?"

Santino didn't move a muscle.

"I'm sorry. Would you like me to shave it off for next time?"

"Yes," in a whisper.

"Really?"

The boy shook his head slowly.

"No? Good. I'm glad that's not necessary because I really like my mustache. But I want you to know I'd be ready to give it up for you."

He took a chair and sat down next to the bed. "Let's get started. Do you remember your first and last name?"

Santino murmured, "Santino Cannetta."

"And your parents?"

"Alfonso and Assunta Cannetta."

It went on like that. Easy questions, his address, how many people in his family, their names, what kind of car his father had. Then the man moved on to questions about parts of the body. He pointed and touched Santino very gently and he had to answer: arm, hand, foot, hair, eyes.

After that he showed him geometrical shapes. A square, a rectangle, a circle. Santino answered all the questions. When he was slow to respond, Assunta urged him on.

"Very good so far. You're a bright boy. Do you like school?"

"No."

"No? You're honest! Excellent. Now tell me, do you know why you're in the hospital?"

Santino mumbled something that sounded like "Shots."

"I didn't get that. Could you repeat it?"

The only response that came from the bed was a yawn.

"Do you know anyone besides me with a mustache? Anyone in your family, your neighbors, maybe a friend of your parents . . . ."

Santino half-closed his eyes, very sleepy. He stiffened slightly, yawned again, then turned on his side. He seemed to be enclosed in an invisible cocoon.

The neuropsychiatrist gestured that he would give in, and stood up. "Signora Assunta, we'll stop here for today," he said calmly. "I'll be back tomorrow. Your son is making an excellent recovery. It's quite normal that he would shield himself from the memory of the trauma."

* * *

A few hours later a policeman appeared at the door. "He's up," he said, turning to someone behind him.

A man and a woman came in. Neither one wore a white coat. Santino was alone; Mamma had gone out to have lunch. He moved around in bed, uneasy.

The woman came toward him with a big smile.

The smile was forced. He could tell right away.

"Hello, Santino, I hear you're doing quite well. We're very pleased. I can see that you're a smart boy. We're here to ask you a few questions."

They were disconnected sentences, with no real warmth. Santino didn't answer.

The woman stood beside his bed, gazing down at him. She bit her thin lips. Santino felt she was studying him with an icy curiosity, the way you study something you need to take apart. He looked away.

"So, do you miss school?" the intruder continued.

Santino turned toward the man. He had remained a few steps behind. He had chestnut hair and a handsome, lean face. His kind dark eyes were fixed on him. He didn't smile, but his serious gaze seemed to take in a great deal. He was a trifle pale, like someone who didn't get enough sun. His jacket and trousers hung loosely on him. He looked too thin for his clothes.

"This is the magistrate who'll be handling your case," said the woman, seeing that Santino was looking at him. "I'm the psychologist."

She didn't say her name, nor that of the magistrate.

"So do you like school?" she inquired again in that stubbornly sweet tone. "School is nice, isn't it? You have so many little friends, and you learn interesting things. I know you must be missing it . . . ."

He gazed dully into space.

The woman turned to the man behind her and remarked in a frightened voice: "He looks like he's been through a war."

Santino shifted around. His war survivor's gaze fixed again on the magistrate. What he glimpsed was a face that was ill at ease, like someone who didn't want to be where he was.

The psychologist went on, coating every single word in honey. "What's the matter, can't you talk? A clever boy like you . . . . Tell us what happened the day you were at the Ghost Town."

Santino closed up like a clam. He shut his eyes and put his good arm on his chest and his hand in front of his face. He curled up and went stiff. Inside the cocoon again.

"We know you're intelligent . . . " continued the fluty voice. "You can resist but we won't give up. Now take that hand away from your face, please, and explain what happened. We have an idea already but we want to hear it from you."

He didn't move. He was waiting for them to go away, to disappear into the world outside and leave him in peace.

Still curled up and not moving, he waited in vain for the sound of the door opening to get rid of them. One of them coughed. It must have been the man.

"Even at that young age, they're already trapped in the Mafia culture," the woman said in a disappointed whisper; the dulcet tones were gone. "They don't talk, even on pain of death." And then, once again in the false voice, "You're not a Mafioso, are you? I know you'll tell us everything."

Santino raised his eyelids with a sly look. No way I'll talk, his look said. I'm no rat. He noticed the magistrate hadn't moved a muscle. He was still staring. His kind eyes seemed to be saying, I wish I didn't have to be here. I wish none of us had to be here. Why had he come if he wasn't going to say a word?

He looked at the woman again and suddenly thought of a way to get rid of her. He looked her up and down the way he he'd seen certain men sitting at the bar in Tonduzzo do when a girl passed. From her neck he moved gradually down to her shoulders, her chest, where he lingered with a sly grin, then proceeded down and ended up at the legs sticking out of the dark suit. Her face wasn't exactly ugly, but her lips were too thin. Her eyes weren't bad. Her hair, black, short, and straight, made her look severe. And she was much too skinny. Paola, the nurse, was much prettier.

Santino didn't know if his tough guy connoisseur look was credible or ridiculous, but he saw the psychologist blush and step back slightly.

She said nothing to him, just spun around toward the man and exclaimed irritably: "It's no use. We won't get anything out of him today. He's rejecting us."

The pair went out in silence, the magistrate slowly following the psychologist. Before he left the room he turned back to flash the child a quick glance that seemed apologetic.

*   *   *

Santino wanted paper and pencil to write to Paola and compliment her. Sitting in bed, using the small hospital table—and ignoring the intravenous drip attached to his arm—he drew a blonde woman with the crayons Uncle Turi had brought him. He drew in freckles, a few on the cheeks, a few in the air around her. Then he wrote: "Paola, will you marry me when I grow up? When I'm all better I'll buy you a ring." He drew two interlocking hearts and signed it.

He showed the drawing to his mother. Assunta was full of praise. For the first time, she gave a small smile. Santino saw that even if she'd become an old woman, her smile was still the same.

Then he wanted to draw more things. Besides the drawing of Paola, none of his scribbles contained any people. The sheets of paper piled up on the table: prehistoric monsters, lions, huge cats that were tigers, a train, a helicopter, a house.

Rocco, one of the two policemen stationed in the hall, appeared in the doorway. Since he'd already made friends with Santino, Assunta took advantage of his visit to go make some calls and get something to eat in the hospital café. She promised to bring back a sweet.

"Look!" Santino said to him.

Rocco came over. "That's really beautiful," he exclaimed with exaggerated enthusiasm. He picked up the drawing of the cottage. "Lucky you, to have a house like that."

"Do you have a *zita*?" the boy asked him.

"Not yet."

"I do."

"Who is it?"

"Paola." He showed him the picture of Paola. "But I also like Teresa and Rosa."

"Cool. So many!"

"But Paola said she would be my *zita*."

"You're a lucky boy."

"She's the best of the best. A ten."

"You're right."

Santino thought for a moment. "But I'm still young. I don't know how long I'll have to wait."

Suddenly his eyes grew blurry, as if someone had poured in a spoonful of fog.

The policeman thought he was about to fall asleep and left the room on tiptoe.

129

*   *   *

There were lots of interviews over the next few days. Guglielmo, the psychiatrist with the mustache, came back with a blonde woman psychologist who was very nice. She was the complete opposite of the one with the tight lips and honeyed voice. He liked her, but she was a little old, not like Paola. They came twice a day.

He had a lot of fun with them. They asked him about his favorite TV programs. And he cheerily rattled off the whole plot of his favorite cartoon—a long, complicated story with lots of characters. It was unusual to find grown-ups who would listen so attentively.

But other times they asked him questions about the horrible thing that had happened at Poggioreale Vecchia, and he immediately lost all desire to speak.

"Don't worry, you're among friends," they said. But he would start to cry and sink into a heavy sleepiness. So he closed his eyes until they left. When Mamma returned, he went back to his drawing.

The silent magistrate came to see him again. This time he was alone; the woman he wouldn't speak to must have been offended.

He took off his jacket and tie like someone not accustomed to wearing them. "I'm Francesco. Do you remember me?" he said as soon as he came in.

Santino was sitting up in bed. Assunta got up from the armchair to leave, but the man stopped her. "Please stay, signora. That way your son will feel more at ease." He spoke with a slight Sicilian accent.

He took a chair and sat down next to the bed. "Hi, Santino. I'm the magistrate who's been assigned your case. Do you know what a magistrate is?"

Santino shook his head timidly.

"It's a person who works for the government. His job is to find murderers and accuse them of the crimes they committed, so they can be put in prison. It's a job I love, you understand?" He was talking to him as if they were friends.

Santino was silent, studying the young yet authoritative face. He decided to nod his head, yes.

"They killed Papa and Nonno," he said in a low voice.

"Yes, I know. The psychiatrist and psychologist who've been talking to you these last few days told me that you can testify if you want to. They said you're intelligent and careful, you understand things, and you have a good memory in spite of everything you went through. That doesn't happen often."

He hadn't even mentioned the skinny psychologist. Even if his words were complicated, he spoke without insisting on a response. He was a soothing presence.

"Kids are like reeds," he was saying, "that bend in the wind, but when the wind stops they straighten up right away. They're flexible, they're able to adapt to difficult situations

131

without suffering too much damage. They're more flexible in this way than adults. In our strange jargon we call this resilience. Though it can happen sometimes, if the gust of wind is too strong, even children will snap. But not you. You straightened right up."

Santino was listening. It didn't bother him too much that he didn't grasp a lot of the words. What he liked was the man's tone: calm, firm, not asking questions. He was talking to him man to man.

"The testimony of a child under six years old, the age when they start to go to school, is usually not too reliable. He can be believed up to a certain point, but you never know if he's making things up or not. But you're older."

Santino looked at him, intrigued.

"You're six and a half."

"Almost seven!" Santino corrected.

"That's right. You're old enough so that your testimony at a trial can be considered usable. We're fortunate in this. If you were younger, if you were five, for instance, your word wouldn't count for much under the law. At that age children still have a vague sense of what's real and what isn't. But you ... you can already tell the difference between reality and fantasy."

He stopped for a moment while Santino digested this important information.

"I know what happened to you. It makes me angry and sad. With your help, I'd like to see that justice is done. But it's not enough that I know: to get justice I need you to tell me what happened. In court your words will be worth more than mine."

The magistrate paused for a moment to make sure the boy had understood. Santino was silent.

"They shot your Papa, your Nonno, and you: this we both know. The judges know it too, the ones who evaluate the proof that I, as magistrate, will gather. But the person who lived through this event has to tell what happened and what he saw. I understand that you don't want to talk about it. I wouldn't either, if I were in your place. But I would feel a responsibility toward the victims. Not for revenge. For justice: to keep the bad people from doing more bad things in the future."

Santino felt a kind of sickness coming on. He liked Francesco, but he shouldn't talk to him because he was a cop. Uncle Turi had said that if he spoke to the cops he would be a lousy rat.

"I don't remember anything," he said in a garbled voice.

"Look at me, Santino. Open your eyes. You know why you're in the hospital."

"I don't know. I don't remember!" A small band of white showed through his lowered eyelids. His face seemed to shrink in pain.

"Speak to the gentleman, my darling," Assunta said. Until that moment she had been so silent that he'd almost forgotten she was in the room.

133

Now she was beside him. "You can tell the magistrate what happened." She stroked his hand quickly. More than a caress, it seemed like a kind of nudge, as if to show him the way.

"I saw a little goat," the boy whispered. "In the Ghost Town." He broke off.

"Go on," said Francesco gently. "I know it's hard."

"I went over to the *capruzza* and there were shots. She ran away."

"And then?"

His face shrank again and the whites of his eyes flickered beneath his lids. His body shuddered. And shuddered again.

"And what did you do?"

"I ran to the gate."

"Yes, the gate."

"Blood. There was so much blood. Papa's back . . . with . . . and Nonno's eyes were like my marbles . . . he didn't see me."

"Were they dead?"

Santino opened his eyes for an instant and turned to Assunta. "You told me Papa and Nonno are in heaven."

"Yes, sweetheart."

"Who else did you see?" Francesco persisted.

"I don't know. I don't remember."

"Was there anyone else?"

"Yes . . . ."

"And you saw him."

"One with a gun." His face contorted again.

"With a gun?"

"No . . . with a pistol."

"Who had the pistol?"

"I don't know."

"And what did you do?"

"I . . . . The shots were coming at me."

"Yes, they shot you. But I need to know *who* shot, so I can put him in prison. So he won't be able to kill anyone else."

"I don't know . . . . I don't know."

"You were wounded in the front, between your shoulder and your heart. So you were facing the man with the pistol. You looked straight at him. The man who killed your father. It was him. We know that from the bullets. The ones the surgeon took out of your body are the same as those from your father's body. Your grandfather was killed with different kinds of bullets. So you can understand that means there was at least one other person. Maybe more. Tell me how many there were."

"Two."

"Who's the one who shot you?"

"Weas . . . el . . . ."

"What? That sounds like an animal."

"I mustn't tell!" With his eyes wide open, Santino started sobbing.

"Listen to me, Santino. Did someone tell you not to talk?"

135

Santino closed his eyes without answering. He had totally given up; his worn-out face was wet with tears and snot. Every now and then a sob shook him. Finally, he was still.

He was fast asleep.

Chapter 18
Lucio

"Mamma, mamma, we're back!" Ilaria shrieks in the living room.

Inside the apartment a woman's voice is singing a Neapolitan song. The radio is on very low. There's no one in the living room.

"Don't yell like a lunatic," I say. "She might be sleeping."

Mamma's not in the master bedroom. The mess I find is very unlike her: the bed is unmade, the closet doors are open. My room is empty too. I knock hard on the bathroom door, then fling it open.

"She went out!" I say in astonishment. "Where could she have gone?"

Ilaria looks at me, her eyes wide. It's the first time in ages that we haven't found our mother at home.

"She went out?" she asks in disbelief, in a piping little voice.

"It looks that way. She must have gone for just a minute. She left the radio on."

I have an idea. I go to my room to hunt for the cell phone I forgot to take with me. I can't find it. That's odd. I thought I left it on the table, where I always keep it when I'm at home. I go back to Mamma's room, rummage through the tangled sheets, and find a cell. Mine. Who knows why she had it? I certainly didn't leave it on her bed.

I call Mamma's number. Now we'll find out where she is. We don't have a landline at home, just the cells.

The telephone rings for a long time, then Ilaria informs me that besides the song on the radio, there's a weak ring coming from somewhere in the living room.

With my phone still on, I return to the living room and follow the rings till I get to the armchair. There's nothing under the cushions, so I look underneath. And there it is. Mamma's cell.

Now, one thing Mamma would never do, not even if the house were invaded by giant cockroaches, is go out. Another thing she would absolutely never do, not even if she was fleeing from a fire, is be without her cell phone. Even if she hardly ever uses it.

I turn off my phone, pick up Mamma's, and stare at it in bewilderment.

"I'm the one who heard it!" Ilaria squeaks shrilly.

"Right, you're a smart girl."

Fear gnaws at me, my throat is dry, I have no saliva. There's a different voice on the radio now, a man's voice. *Paloma*. I recognize the song.

In between the throbbing tones, I try to think. Our next-door neighbor, Agnese, is the only person in the building Mamma has any contact with. Maybe she went to borrow some butter, bread, an aspirin? Or just for a quick visit?

"Go ring Agnese's bell," I tell Ilaria.

"Why me?"

"Go on. I bet if you stand on tiptoe you can reach the bell."

"But why do *I* have to go?"

"Because maybe Mamma's there," I say hoarsely.

While Ilaria's out on the landing, I examine Mamma's cell. If she called someone, it would come up in calls sent. In fact there is one call, made at 4:38. She called me. That explains the mystery of my phone on her bed. When it rang in my room, she must have realized that I'd forgotten to take it. She insists, whenever I'm out with Ilaria, that I always have it with me. Now I bet all hell will break loose.

I look for other calls: there's one from yesterday, also to me. Incoming calls: one from me three days ago. I search the messages. Maybe she sent me a text? No.

I click away, my ear tense from the prolonged ring of the doorbell. Ilaria's pressing it doggedly and that metallic sound coming from the landing works its way into the voice singing on the radio.

Did she get sick and the neighbors called an ambulance? That's another possibility.

There's a text on her phone. I open it. On the little screen are the words: "Your mother is dying. Come to Palermo right away."

Only those words. No signature.

This text, which Mamma must have read, makes my fingers and toes cramp up. It was sent at 4:36. Two minutes before she called me. So she was trying to reach me after getting that message.

I look for the number that those strange words came from: they don't give me a clue. Who wrote to tell us that Nonna is dying?

Ilaria's back. "No one came to the door. Should I go downstairs and ring?"

I stop her with a hand. "Wait."

My heart is racing wildly. I'm afraid to do what I'm about to do. But I have to, if I want to find out anything.

I call the number in Palermo that the message came from. Three rings, four, then an old man's phlegmy voice answers, calls me by my name, and adds, "Come right away, please!"

I immediately push the red button to hang up. I can't breathe. My head is spinning. He used *my* name.

It's a trap! A trap!

It can't be Nonno—he's dead. Panic wraps me up in a black cloak that cuts off the air. I'm suffocating. I'm losing my mind. Suddenly I'm whirling around like a dervish. Why? I don't know. Maybe to wake myself up from this awful dream. Or to drop down dead. From a great distance, I hear the final notes of *Paloma*.

"What's the matter with you?" Ilaria screams. "What is it?"

I stop suddenly and look at her. I must be terrifying her, my eyes must look wild, like I'm possessed by demons. She steps back in alarm.

I try to gather some saliva in my mouth so I can speak.

"They kidnapped Mamma," I announce in a thick voice.

"What?"

"They took her away."

"Who?"

Now Ilaria's sobbing.

"The Russians." I look around, baffled. "We've got to get away from here, fast. This minute!"

"Why did they take her away?" A shiver runs through her small body under the pink dress, all creased now.

"Remember the story I told you? How Papa is a scientist and the Russians are after his formula? That's why they kidnapped Mamma. They believe she has it."

"What will they do to her?"

"I don't know. But they'll keep her alive, and when they realize she doesn't have the formula they'll come after me."

"Did they take her to Russia with them? Is she with Papa now?"

"Maybe."

"Let's turn on the TV," she says, like a sensible child. "They'll say who kidnapped her and we'll see where they took her." She gets the remote, ready to press the button.

"No, I don't think so, Illy. Let it alone."

Ilaria drops her arm and starts crying again. "What . . . What'll we do?"

I don't answer. I know I look feverish, hardly reassuring, but I just can't change my expression. There's no time to comfort my sister. I need to think.

I know where Mamma keeps her money. If they carried her off in a rush, as the radio left on and the unmade bed suggest, she couldn't have taken the hidden money. On the other hand, if the *picciuli* aren't there, maybe she left on her own. I open the dresser drawer and unfold her long woolen stockings. Inside is the roll of bills, untouched. Without counting them, I stuff them in my pocket together with the money she gave us for lunch.

Mamma didn't leave of her own free will.

"Let's get out of here! Hurry up!" I shout harshly.

Speechless with fear, Ilaria seizes the bag she had at the beach, the one with her towel, her wet bathing suit, and her plastic water wings.

"No, you don't need that. Just take a light sweater."

She obeys.

I grab my jacket. Meanwhile I think furiously. To get out, it's best to go up to the roof and climb over the low wall that separates it from the roof of the condo next door. From there we can get to another staircase and go out through the neighboring building, which opens onto a side street. In case someone's waiting for us outside the house.

I've already opened the door when I get another idea. "Wait here," I tell Ilaria, and dash into my room.

In thirty seconds I'm back. "Let's go."

I follow the escape route I planned, dragging Ilaria by the hand. She stumbles with every step as if she's forgotten how to walk. We don't meet anyone. On the roof next door I stop short. Ilaria stares at me, panicked.

"The radio. We left it on." I shrug. "Never mind."

We continue with our escape.

Once we're outside, we walk in the direction opposite to our street. When we're far enough away and I'm fed up with Ilaria's stumbling, I say excitedly, "Isn't this a fabulous adventure? You and I are the brave heroes. We're fleeing from the bad Russians to save our mother. You know, don't you, that the good heroes always, always win?"

Ilaria doesn't nod her head as I hoped. She just whimpers softly, under her breath, looking down at the ground. She wants her Mamma, and that's all there is to it.

Chapter 19

Santino

Many people came and went in Santino's room each day. Uncle Turi visited often and tried every trick in the book to be alone with his nephew. The only one who didn't show up was his grandmother, who was too old and frail to leave the house. Mamma slept there all the time, on an armchair that opened into a cot at night.

The nurses came to change him, to bring his meals and disinfect his wounds. Paola had already received three letters from Santino, who had written to Teresa and Rosa as well. In the halls they couldn't stop talking about the miracle child. He'd become the hospital mascot. The police officers peeked in and sometimes came inside to have a chat. Talking to them distracted Santino.

His meetings with the psychiatrist and psychologist, on the other hand, made him get serious. Endless sketches about the location of the two figures on the square, detailed questions, memory tests. He was smart, he knew, but the sketches were very far-fetched.

And then there was the magistrate. Despite the anxiety these visits caused, Santino realized he looked forward to them with pleasure.

Francesco would sit down next to the bed and explain to him how the Mafia worked, how the Mafiosi took protection money from all the storekeepers and businesses, threatening that otherwise they'd burn down their stores. How they thought nothing of snuffing out human lives with the same nonchalance as putting out a cigarette or turning off a car engine. "I 'took out' so and so," they'd say. I took out some dude. I killed him. They had the nerve to justify their behavior, saying it was to protect citizens because the State couldn't do it. And they called themselves "men of honor."

They thought they were the State.

A State that kills.

But it wasn't true that the State was made up of Mafiosi.

"Are the men in the real State all good? Even the cops?" Santino asked one day. These were complex discussions and he needed to understand.

Francesco gave a tight little smile. "Yes, the cops are honest people. But the Mafiosi tell everyone that they're bad. Enemies."

One morning when Francesco seemed more determined than usual, he explained why the witnesses and the victims who survived didn't dare to speak out.

"This collective silence is called *omertà*," he said. "It's part of Sicilian culture. We Sicilians inherit it from generation to generation. From the minute we learn to walk we learn that we always keep our affairs to ourselves. Eyes don't see, ears don't hear. If you talk, you're a rat. Even you know that word, I bet."

Santino flinched. He nodded.

Francesco seemed not to notice. He went on heatedly. "*Omertà* comes above all from fear: fear of being killed by the Mafia, fear that they'll burn your house, fear for your family. It's a huge fear. But you don't have to have this fear, Santino. We're protecting you, and we'll keep on protecting you in the future."

He repeated this every time he came to see him. "We'll protect you; you have to trust us. We're on your side. I won't let anyone hurt you."

Santino wasn't convinced. Even if he trusted Francesco, even if he was sure no one would "take him out" because the officers outside his door wouldn't let any strangers enter, he still didn't want to be a rat.

"I don't remember," was his reply.

Despite the monotony of hospital life, the days passed quickly. When the police returned the bodies to the family, Assunta went to the funerals of her husband and father. She left Santino with Paola, the nurse with the freckles. Santino cried in the nurse's arms for a long time while he waited for his mother to return.

"Now you're all I have left, my sweetheart," his mother said when she came back from the cemetery. "My little man, my life . . . ." She broke out in heartrending sobs until Paola drew her gently away and hugged her tight.

* * *

They removed his bandages and his cast. He got out of bed and managed to hop around the room on crutches.

He didn't ask what would happen next. He drew and kept writing letters to the nurses. He talked with Mamma. He had never been so pampered. Sometimes Assunta would sing him an old lullaby very softly, and Santino felt like he was little again, touching the damp maternal breast. Then something in him rebelled and he asked her to sing *Ciuri Ciuri*.

Assunta began in thin, uncertain tones, but she quickly gathered energy and the lively Sicilian rhythm filled the little room.

> *Ciuri ciuri, ciuri*
> *Di tutu l'annu*
> *L'amuri ca mi dasti*
> *ti lu turnu . . . .*

Santino smiled. Flowers, flowers all year long, the love you gave me I give back to you. It was as if roses and cyclamen and mimosa and tulips and orange blossoms were coming in through the window.

Francesco often appeared to interrupt these idylls. Assunta would shut up right away, embarrassed. In a way Santino didn't like that, and in a way he was glad.

The crutches were soon set aside.

And then came one morning when the magistrate entered looking more serious and determined than usual. "Hello, Santino," he said and, wasting no time, pulled up a chair next to where he was sprawled out.

"*Ciao*," he mumbled, made wary by that determined look.

Francesco turned to Assunta. Without a word, he made a sign for her to leave the room.

"Today you and I need to have an important talk. Do you know the doctors say you're all better? You can leave here. Are you glad?"

Santino gave a slight nod. In fact he felt scared at the thought of leaving that room.

"Before leaving the hospital you have to make a decision. You're at a turning point, my friend. Whether you like it or not, you must make a choice. I want to talk to you like a grown-up. Listen carefully. There are two possibilities."

Santino was very attentive. There was something different in Francesco's face. No soothing, no affectionate smiles, no jokes. He didn't address him as a kid; he was truly talking to him like an adult.

148

"The Mafia is evil and must be fought. This you already know. It seems invincible, but it isn't, because it's made up of people like us. No group of people that uses evil as a weapon is invincible, if you really want to defeat it. But it takes people who are passionate and struggle for life as intensely as they struggle for destruction and death."

He spoke with emphasis, as Santino had never heard him do before. He stared at the magistrate in bewilderment.

Francesco smiled; his stern face softened. "I'm not the one who said these things. It was Gandhi. Do you know who Gandhi was?"

"No."

"Gandhi was an Indian man who fought with all his being. He struggled for just causes, without ever using violence."

"My papa wasn't violent either. He never beat me."

"I believe you. Your father was a fine man, not a Mafioso. He might have stolen to feed your family, but he never hurt anyone. I'm sure of that. And your grandfather never hurt a fly. But they didn't have the strength to expose the Mafiosi they were mixed up with. They thought they'd be protected, and instead they were killed by them. Your papa and Nonno must have made some kind of mistake."

"They wanted to get money for my first communion." The words escaped Santino with a sigh.

Francesco gazed at him in silence for a moment. "Money for your first communion. And for that they were murdered.

149

Don't you understand that such ruthless people have to be put away somewhere secure where they can't do any more evil?"

At that moment Santino envied the cop, though in a confused way. He envied his conviction of what was just and what was not, his will to fight the forces of evil, his courage. The magistrate risked his life every day. He'd once confided in him, during one of their talks, that he had to go around with a police escort. Many cops die fighting the Mafia. Santino would have liked to be like him, think like him, have his courage.

"If you tell me their names," Francesco resumed, "we can have a fair trial of your father and grandfather's killers. If instead you decide to keep silent, we can't do anything but let them go free to carry on, because we won't have decisive proof. We've caught one of them, because we had clues that made it possible: your grandfather's bloody shirt was found in his house. He'd washed it, but with luminol the stains showed up."

"What's luminol?" Santino asked, very upset.

"It's a substance that lets you see stains that you can't see with the naked eye. We knew very well that he was a Mafioso, but we couldn't keep him for long without this proof. We don't know who the other one is. But you were looking right at him."

"Yes," whispered Santino, his eyes wide with a private and horrid vision. "I saw them."

He understood that he was wrong not to be on the side of justice. He wanted them to be punished, even at the cost of his own life, because they were the wicked rats. Them, not him.

"Who are they?"

Curled up in the armchair, his feet dangling over the edge, not touching the floor, he looked around the room. "Are there any microphones here?" he asked.

"Microphones? In this room? No, we haven't put any here. Why? Did you think there were any?"

"In films they always have them." He didn't want him to know that Uncle Turi had inspected the room and whispered in his ear.

"Did you know them? Did you know the killers?"

"One of them."

"What's his name?" Francesco asked calmly, looking him straight in the eye.

"Weasel."

"What kind of name is that? Is it a nickname?"

"He has a mustache like a weasel. That's the name I thought up for him when I was younger." Santino gave a forced smile, aware that he hadn't given away anything essential.

"So that's why you were scared of Gigli's mustache, the psychiatrist! Do you know this Weasel's real name?"

He thought it over. Could he really tell it? Betray someone? Would Mamma be mad? In his uncertainty, he gave a yawn.

The magistrate stood up. "I see you don't want to. Okay then, it'll just take us longer to find your father's murderer."

He moved toward the door. A voice, barely more than a breath, reached him in the doorway.

"*U Taruccatu.*"

Francesco turned back.

"That sounds like a nickname too. Did you give it to him?"

"No . . . not me. They did."

"Do you know his real name? If you don't it's okay, we can see who's called *u Taruccatu* in Mafia circles. We'll surely find him, but it will take time, and time is precious for those of us hunting him."

Santino felt he was facing a boundary line: a major dividing line after which his life would change forever. He was suspended between two worlds. He searched inside himself to see if Mamma would approve of what he wanted to do. Then he realized that he had to decide himself, regardless of what Mamma thought. He himself, all on his own, had to cross that perilous line.

He straightened up in the armchair, putting his feet on the floor, his hands clutching the armrests. His shoulder still hurt and his knee was stiff, but he felt a new strength inside.

"Pasquale Loscataglia," he said in a clear voice, looking straight at Francesco.

Now there was relief in his eyes. As if he had let a terrible weight fall from his back.

"Don Ciccio's son and heir, the boss of the Loscataglias!"

The magistrate had lost his imperturbable calm. He looked like an excited kid. He ran a hand over his hair.

"We've been hunting Don Ciccio for years, but he's a fugitive. He's very well hidden, the *Scannapopulu.** You see, even we know this boss's nickname. So it was his son who shot you! Do you know where he lives?"

"No. No one at home knew. He used to come to our house . . . or Papa met him outside somewhere."

"It doesn't matter, since he must have left his regular home. And the other one, the one who killed your grandfather?"

"I don't know the other. I never saw him before."

"We're sure it's the one we arrested, who's awaiting trial in the Ucciardone prison. This afternoon I'll show you photos. We'll see if you recognize him. That would be the final confirmation. You've been great, Santino. You've done what many adults I've met in my work have never had the courage to do."

Santino sank back into the armchair. It was over. He felt emptied out, utterly exhausted. Yet full of a calm he'd never felt before. He'd done the right thing, like in the Westerns where the bad guy goes over to the good guys. Though he usually goes back to his old life.

"You think that now they'll kill me?"

---

* *Scannapopulu*: someone who commits many murders and terrifies people.

"Absolutely not. You'll be completely protected by the police, Santino. Forever."

He asked again, faintly, "If I live, do you think when I'm grown up I could be a cop?"

Francesco smiled. "Would you like to?"

"Yes."

"You could even become a magistrate or a judge, if that's what you want. You have the right stuff. But I'm afraid you'll have to get to like school a bit more."

Chapter 20
Lucio

I keep running, dragging Ilaria by the hand, with no idea where we're going. My thoughts are swirling around in my head like a whirlwind, all tangled and chaotic.

One of them is hammering at me. The text comes from Palermo. It says: "Your mother is dying."

It would take a strong motive, something really dramatic, to convince Mamma to return to Palermo. Such as the news that her mother is near death. But somehow I have a sense that it's not true that Nonna is dying. I don't know why, but that's how I feel.

It's a very carefully planned trap.

But who could know about Mamma's promise? Who could have overheard it? Who? One name comes to mind—a person very close. Someone who could have informed *them*. It might have happened like that.

How did whoever kidnapped Mamma find us? I'll think about this later—for now it's not important.

155

I have to get to Palermo and look for her there. But I won't go where *they* think I would. I'll look for the Hunter, talk to him. *They'd* never dream I would do that. No, they certainly wouldn't expect that.

Now I need to consider urgent matters, such as where can I leave Ilaria? It's pointless to have her go with me to Palermo, and it's dangerous. Monica is in Sardinia with her family. The neighbors down the hall aren't there. Who, then?

No one comes to mind.

I have no idea where to leave her. And yet . . . my sister isn't a package I can simply drop off somewhere. She would cry so hard she'd have convulsions. Without Mamma, she needs me around just like the air she breathes. Only I can calm her down. Only I understand her inside and out. I understand her even better than our mother.

I'll have to take her with me.

With this settled, I've got to decide where we should go. We get on a bus. I peek anxiously out the windows. The city and the people passing by make me nervous—I wish Ilaria and I were invisible.

I have my cell phone and also Mamma's, which has the number of the old man in Palermo, even if I have no intention of calling him. *They* have a ton of ways to trace where calls come from. They're better at that than the police. Maybe that's just what they expect: that I'll make a call and they'll trace me. My other call must not have worked because I hung up too fast. But anyway, I'll give that number to the Hunter.

"Where are we going?" Ilaria asks shakily. Her red traffic-light cheeks are back, but not from the cold. We're both dripping with sweat.

I lean down to whisper in her ear: "To the port."

I wonder again if it wouldn't be better to go back to Dr. Gaetani, the psychologist. But she would immediately notify the Livorno police. Then the two of us would be shut up in some room to wait while the police handled things.

I don't like that idea. The police always use too many weapons. Mamma's a hostage. It could end in disaster.

"You know what we'll do? We'll take a boat and go to the Hunter," I tell Ilaria, leaning my head on hers again. "He'll find her."

"Who is the Hunter?"

"My best friend."

"You're making him up!"

"Why would I do that?"

"You never told me about him." She seems hurt.

"He's really tough; he knows how to deal with the Russians—he knows them well, and how they operate. He can smoke them out."

Ilaria pushes me away with a sullen look. I'm not sure she believes me.

"He's my best friend," I repeat. "I trust him one hundred percent."

We get off the bus. I know the Mediceo Port well. It's where the ferries leave from. I look around frantically. Ilaria, gripping my hand, sucks her thumb.

It occurs to me that the kidnappers most likely left Livorno by car. If you have a prisoner you don't take a boat where everyone can see you. You leave unobtrusively in a car. Or does Mamma really think they're taking her to her dying mother, so she went along with them without protesting? No, she'd never go without us. Besides, she would have understood immediately that they were crooks. Maybe they tied her up and gagged her and stuck her in the trunk. I have to keep these thoughts to myself—Ilaria is scared enough already.

I stop a woman and ask where the ticket booth for Palermo is.

"For Palermo? Down there. Where it says LARGE FAST BOATS."

We find the ticket booth. There's a short line, and we wait silently. My heart is pounding. When it's my turn I step up and ask in a clear, firm voice: "What time is the boat for Palermo?"

"Today?"

"Yes, today."

The ticket seller speaks without looking at me, his head bent over his papers. "At 11:59." He looks up for an instant but doesn't seem surprised to find himself facing a twelve-year-old boy. "Do you understand? One minute before midnight. The trip is nineteen hours. Round trip?"

"Only one way, two people. One is a child." I don't dare ask if I can get a reduced fare too: I want him to think I'm doing an errand for my parents.

"Deck chair? Inside cabin? Outside cabin?"

"Deck chair." It sounds like the cheapest.

He tells me the price. Luckily the *picciuli* rolled up in the secret pocket of my vest seem to be enough. I carefully extract the right amount from the roll and put away the rest.

The man gives me two tickets and points to the pier where we should board.

It's seven now. We have to wait five hours, less one minute. We'd better buy something to eat at the café and find a place where we can stay safely until close to midnight.

*   *   *

We hurriedly get sandwiches and Cokes and I lead Ilaria toward the New Pier. I remember that at the end of the long platform surrounding the Port there's a row of old sheds separated from the pier by a fence. They look like an abandoned train, with dilapidated cars. That's where I'm planning for us to hide to wait out the five hours. Those sheds can't have been used for years.

We get to the fence—the pier is deserted here. It's just used in the morning or early afternoon by people who come to fish. But we have to hurry.

I get us past the fence through a low rusty gate. The windows of the shed are made of lots of small glass squares, half of them missing. I peek inside. There's a pile of stuff on the ground, but in the dark I can't tell what it is. We can't get in through the windows because the broken squares and the good ones are held together by an iron grating. I try a door made of planks of rotted wood. With one strong heave of my shoulder it goes creak-creak. Another heave and there's a louder creaking. At the third, a few boards give way and fall off. There's a space big enough for us to pass through.

From where I stand in the doorway, it's dark inside and smells of mildew. Ilaria steps back. "It's a perfect hiding place," I say, and push her inside.

In the faint light I can see what's on the ground: ropes, old anchors, shovels, pieces of iron, rotting sails. From the corner of my eye I catch sight of a small dark animal that darts away, vanishing into the shadows. A rat? Better not tell Ilaria. I try to rearrange the planks that came off the door as best I can: it's a makeshift job. I hope no one passes by.

We settle in an empty corner and I quickly take out the Coke, open it, and offer it to Ilaria.

"There's no straw," she complains.

"Drink it from the can," I tell her brusquely. Right away I regret my harsh tone and I smile, handing her a ham and cheese sandwich.

We eat slowly, in silence. There's plenty of time: five hours. We're more or less safe here. When we're done eating, I roll up my vest and put it on the ground.

"Use it as a pillow," I tell Ilaria.

She obeys without protest and stretches out. In the dim light of the shed, she looks pale. Her thumb is in her mouth again. After a few minutes she closes her eyes.

It's very hot in here. But soon it'll be evening and we'll feel better. I stretch out too. For a pillow I take some coiled-up rope.

I feel around in my pants pocket. Touching the wood of the Indian knife gives me courage. It was a good idea to go back and get it before we left. It's a weapon. And I need some protection.

I lie awake thinking. I mustn't fall asleep. No matter what, we can't miss that ferry. I'll have to keep an eye on my watch.

Ilaria snores lightly. I'm alone, and my thoughts rush in like galloping horses. Memories of the Hunter. The man who changed my life.

Chapter 21
Santino

The day before the most famous patient on the floor got permission to leave the hospital, Francesco came to see him with a black folder under his arm.

He found Santino alone in his room.

He quickly opened the black folder to show him an album full of photographs. There were fifteen close-ups of grim faces. Without hesitation, Santino pointed his finger at the photo of Pasquale and the other man, the one he'd never seen before the ambush.

"Are you sure?"

"I'm sure."

But that wasn't all.

The day before, Francesco had already explained to Assunta: "Before we relocate you, Santino has to come to the courthouse for the official identification. The court requires this, even if he's recognized the murderers from the booking photos. He has to see them in person, behind a one-way mirror."

Then he turned to the boy and reminded him gently that he had to make the identification.

"The way it works is, on their side, they'll see just an ordinary mirror, but on our side this mirror is a transparent window."

"I know. I saw that in a film on TV."

"Good," Francesco exclaimed. "So you don't need to be afraid."

But Santino wasn't at all reassured.

"I don't want to see them close up!"

"You need to. It'll be your last test. It's called an evidentiary hearing. I know they're hard words, but all they mean is that you won't be called to testify during the trial because you've already made the identification at the lineup. Trials can go on for a long time, you know—they've got to get the lawyers, the public prosecutor, the judge, and the jury all together. It can take ages. But you won't need to be bothered; you don't have to appear at the trial."

"What's the public prosecutor?" Santino asked.

"The person who represents the State and gathers evidence against the alleged criminals."

"What?"

"I'm sorry, I keep forgetting you can't know these legal terms. The alleged criminals are the ones suspected of a crime. Murder is a crime."

"I know that!"

"Good. The lawyers, on the other hand, are on the side of the accused."

"Who accuses the bad guys?"

"In your case? Do you think that I'd let anyone else handle your case?"

"No . . . ."

"It's me!"

Santino regarded him with relief. "If it's you, then I'm sure you'll throw them in prison."

"Let's hope so. The Mafia lawyers are cunning, and one of the accused is in hiding, a fugitive."

*   *   *

Right after Francesco left, Paola, the young nurse with the freckles, came into the hospital room. She was carrying a small package wrapped in blue gauze, which she held out to the boy.

Confetti, Santino thought happily. He straightened up in the armchair to take it. But the small package didn't feel like confetti—more like something hard.

He looked at Paola, who was smiling.

"It's your medallion with the trinacria," she said. "I saved it for you. I thought that now that you're better it won't scare you anymore."

Santino suppressed the grimace he was about to make
and nodded weakly.

"I bet you want it back now, your charm. What do you
say? It might even have saved your life."

Santino nodded again, drearily.

"Should I help you put it around your neck?"

"I'll do it later."

He didn't want to hurt her feelings. He twisted around
to stick the little package in his shorts pocket and thanked
her politely.

"I'll miss you. Hospital life is so boring. You've cheered
me up. Did I tell you that I hung your drawings up in my
house? Everyone says it's impossible that a boy of your
age made them. You must be very talented." She embraced
him gently.

"You're the most beautiful one of all," said Santino. "The
best of the best."

The woman laughed kindly, and Santino realized she
really would be sad to see him go.

The pager in the nurse's pocket buzzed. Paola ran out
of the room, throwing him a kiss. Santino sat very still in
his armchair, thinking. Then he got up and hobbled into
the bathroom.

He needed something heavy. He looked around. The
tooth glass was plastic. Everything in the bathroom was
plastic. He went back into the room. The cart with his
breakfast hadn't been removed yet. He studied it.

The metal tray on top of it looked suitable. He picked it up. It was very heavy.

Carrying it back into the bathroom wasn't easy. He took the package out of his pocket and thought of opening it, but he didn't. He placed it on the stone floor, bent over, and dropped the tray on it with all his might. The more he banged, the more furious he grew. He was so worked up that he didn't care about making too much noise. His arms ached from the exertion.

Finally, exhausted and bathed in sweat, he paused to touch the package with his finger. Whatever was in there was smashed to pieces by now. Just for good measure he banged on it a few more times, but with less energy. He stood up with the crushed package in his hand. Now even his leg hurt from all that crouching down. He untied the tiny silk laces and held the blue gauze with its contents over the water. He hit it a few times so that the remains of the amulet Pasquale had given him fell into the bowl. Finally, after a slight hesitation, he threw in the empty wrapping. He didn't want anything that had touched the cursed charm, even if it came from Paola.

He flushed, and with a mean smile watched the last shards get sucked down the drain.

*   *   *

Once he was declared better by all the doctors who'd seen him, with teary eyes Santino said goodbye to the policemen and nurses and left the hospital with his mother and Francesco.

He limped to the police car and got in. Now that the moment had almost come, the complicated language of the courts whirled around in his head as he tried to make sense of the words. The car was nearing the place where he would see his grandfather's killer.

He grew more and more anxious. He started kicking against the seat in front of him. The police escort was in the front with the driver, and he, Mamma, and Francesco sat in the back.

Before he knew it they were in front of the courthouse. The word JUSTICE blazed forth above the broad entrance in letters carved in stone.

Santino didn't want to get out, but finally, with a big sigh, he poked out a leg.

"What if I don't recognize him?"

"If you can't identify him you must say so," said Francesco calmly. "No one is forcing you to recognize anyone."

Mamma added, "I'll be right near you, my love, you mustn't worry."

"No, I'm sorry, signora, we can't do that. You'll have to wait outside the room. Your being there could influence Santino."

Assunta attempted a laugh. "See how important you are to the magistrate? You're the only one he wants."

Before passing through the great, wide-open door, Santino stopped suddenly. He turned to look at the strange monument in the middle of the courtyard.

"What's that green stone thing?" he asked.

"It's not stone; it's bronze. It has two wings, you see? It represents Dike, goddess of Justice."

Santino took some more time to look around. "That's the Italian flag on that balcony," he noted.

"That's right."

He lowered his glance to the steps surrounding the courtyard where the two wings flared out.

A name and a date were carved on every step. He began reading them out aloud: "Paolo Borsellino 1992, Francesca Morvillo 1992, Giovanni Falcone 1992, Rosario Livatino 1990, Antonino Saetta, 1988 . . . ."

There were too many. He stopped.

Francesco explained: "They're all men and women who were officers of the law and were killed because of their work. They all sacrificed themselves to fight the power of the Mafia."

"Why are their names on the steps?"

"To remember them. We should never forget the people who gave up their lives to bring peace to this mistreated island. Forgetting them would be like killing them all over again." Francesco shook his head vehemently, as if he regretted getting so carried away.

Santino looked alarmed. "Would you give up your life too?"

"Santù, what kind of question is that!" Assunta burst out.

The magistrate was back to his usual calm self. "I'm very, very careful," he replied with a mild smile. "I can be smarter than they are. Come on, be brave, we're going in now."

Santino did something he'd never done before. He took Francesco's hand; in his other hand he squeezed Mamma's. Pressed between the two of them as in the middle of a sandwich, he had a strange sensation, like something he'd felt before. He felt safe.

They entered the courthouse lobby and then came to a small room. Santino had to let go of Mamma's hand while they waited.

Then, holding Francesco's hand through long corridors, he was taken into the room with the special window.

There were already two men there whom he'd never seen before. The magistrate explained that one was the judge and the other was the lawyer defending the accused. The mysterious glass was completely covered by a lowered shutter. Santino couldn't see anything.

He studied the lawyer with apprehension. A scrawny fellow, pale, with glasses and rounded shoulders. When the two men realized they were being scrutinized, they smiled foolishly.

Santino knew that that man was against him—he struck him as pathetic, to be on the side of the bad guys.

Francesco noticed the boy's frightened glance. He whispered to him: "It's okay. The lawyer doesn't have the right to say a word in here. He can just watch, that's all." Then, looking at the small witness, he realized that he was too short to reach the window. "We need a chair," he declared.

A stool was brought in and put under the window. The lawyer's dull gaze followed every move.

Santino climbed up.

"Ready?" Francesco asked.

"Yes."

The light went out.

In the dark, standing on the stool, he heard the shutter going up; it revealed a lighted room. Three men stood behind the glass, facing in his direction.

Santino's heart began pounding violently, as if it wanted to leap out of his rib cage and flee as far away as possible.

"Don't be scared of their eyes—they can't see you. They're just looking at themselves, because there's a mirror facing them," Francesco reminded him. "Do you recognize anyone?"

"That big one . . . ."

"Which one?"

"In the middle, I think . . . no. The face is different. I never saw him before."

"You're sure?"

"Yes."

"Let's continue."

The shutter closed and immediately the light went on. Francesco and the judge were muttering to each other. The lawyer went over to them and said something. Santino was too upset to listen to their conversation.

They tried again. Again Santino climbed up on the stool. It all went like the first time. After the light went out the shutter rose and three other men appeared, facing front.

"Do they know we're looking at them?" asked Santino.

"Yes, they know."

"Can they hear us?"

"No, they can't."

Santino looked again, concentrating.

"I don't know them."

"You've never seen them before?"

"No."

There was a brief pause after the shutter was lowered again and the light went on. Santino stayed on the stool. No one spoke.

Then the whole thing was repeated for the third time.

"Do you recognize anyone?"

"That one!" Santino shouted right away. "It's him!"

"Which one?"

"The one who was standing near the car. I think it's him because he's big and scary . . . . No, wait, it isn't . . . . Can we go back?"

"Of course. Which ones do you want to see again?"

"The first three."

A few minutes passed and the shutter rose again on the three men who were there the first time.

Santino lingered on them for a long time in silence.

"Take as much time as you need," said the judge. "We're not in any hurry."

"It's him."

"Which one?"

"I was mistaken before," murmured the boy. "It's the one who's big as an ogre, but he has no beard now. He had one before."

"Do you mean that when you saw him during the shooting he had a beard?"

"Yes. He had his back to me, but then he turned around and I saw his beard."

Santino got down from the stool. He was on the verge of falling because of his stiff leg. Francesco caught him.

"Are you sure it's him?"

"Yes. I was confused because he had a beard before. It's him."

"The man you just picked out is Tonio Salsarella, the one we already put in jail because of the drops of blood on his shirt." Francesco seemed relieved. "Now we can keep him in prison until the trial is over. That's good. We're all finished."

The lawyer didn't say anything. His lips were shut tight as if to keep from speaking.

"Isn't *u Taruccatu* here?" the young witness asked in wonder. "Aren't you going to show me Pasquale?"

"I said you wouldn't be able to see him in person, remember? Don Ciccio's son is a fugitive just like his father.

He ran away. Now he's hiding somewhere, maybe in his father's lair or some hideout of his own. They're like wild animals—they get cunning and wary, their ears always on the alert. A few of them, the most brazen, may dare to venture out on the streets where everyone can see them. They know no one will talk, no one will say they saw them. It's like a game for them. Playing a joke on the government. They want us to think they're stronger than we are, that the cops are nothing to them."

Francesco spoke excitedly, his eyes indignant as if at a personal insult. He was about to continue when Santino interrupted.

"He always came to our house on a Kawasaki Z750."

"Ah. Unfortunately I don't think he'd be so foolish as to use that same bike after the ambush. He must have gotten rid of it a while ago. We'll look for it anyway; if we find whoever bought it from him, that might lead somewhere."

"Yes, you might catch him that way."

"I'll hunt him down till we get him," the magistrate promised. "You recognized his photo, and I'll never give up. Never. I won't rest until I put handcuffs on the guy who killed your papa and tried to take out a boy as special as you."

Santino stared at the shutter covering the window. He couldn't get over the fact that a moment ago, Nonno Mico's killer had stood there, in the flesh.

* * *

After they said goodbye to the judge and the lawyer, Francesco took Santino and his mother into his own office.

"What do we do now?" asked Assunta as the door closed behind them. She was very agitated. She twisted her hands. "Now that he's talked, will they kill this boy of mine? He's all I have left."

"We have a witness protection program, signora," said the magistrate. "I already told you about it a few times, and you accepted. You even signed a paper, remember?"

Looking confused, she nodded yes.

"It's already settled that you two will never set foot in Tonduzzo again. A car will take you straight from the courthouse to the airport and from there the Minister of Justice's private plane will take you to a secret location, a northern city. You'll have new identities. You'll both be given new documents with different names."

"And what will we live on?" asked the mother, downcast.

"I was just getting to that. The government will give you a suitable apartment and a monthly subsidy. Santino will have the support of a court psychologist in the city you're going to, because a trauma like his, if it isn't treated, leaves scars. Also the physical therapist for his leg will be paid for by the government. You can apply to the offices of the witness protection program anytime you need anything.

They'll also advise you what to say to your neighbors and to Santino's teachers. They'll make up a plausible story that accounts for your moving."

"But they'll know right away that we're Sicilian," Assunta cried.

"That's true. You can't hide your accent. So, you'll still be Sicilians."

"What city are we going to?" Santino asked, still troubled by the confrontation a little while ago. This latest news about going to live on the mainland took him by surprise.

"I don't know where you're going, and I don't want to know," Francesco answered with a smile. "I won't even know your new last name. For security. Only the people in the witness protection program will know that."

"But I want to write you a note!" Santino protested. "How can you answer me if you don't know where I live?"

The magistrate bent over him. "You can't do that, I'm sorry to say. I could tell from the postmark where you are. It's for your safety. It's so no one can get to you, do you see? It's true that fugitives almost never leave Sicily: they tend to stay where they have relatives and friends who can protect them in their secret hideouts."

"So then it isn't dangerous if we write to each other," Santino retorted stubbornly.

"It's better not to rely on that. The Mafia has men everywhere, men who aren't fugitives, ready to kill on command. We can't write to each other, but I'll never forget you."

"And my mother?" blurted out Assunta, who had suddenly grasped what an enormous change this would make in their lives.

"She can go too. We don't think she's in any danger; the Mafia wouldn't bother hurting such an old woman, who you've told me is also deaf. Not even for revenge. The Mafia always kill with a specific goal in mind. But Signora Nunzia can go with you if she wants to. In fact, I've already thought about her." He cast a glance at the clock. "I asked her to come here at eleven thirty. It's almost eleven now. She'll be here in half an hour. Turi will drive her."

At that name, Santino went pale.

There was a pause while coffee and brioches and an orangeade were brought to the office.

"Can we choose our new names?" Santino asked.

"Not your last name, no," Francesco said. "But if you like you can choose a first name. It'll be easier for you to remember it if it's a name you like, that means something to you."

"I want to be . . . I want to be called . . . Lucio! I really like Lucio!"

"Lucio. So it'll be Lucio. It's a nice name, easy to remember. And you," the magistrate asked Assunta.

She hesitated. Santino spoke for her. "Mamma will be called Bianca," he stated firmly.

"Bianca?" she asked. "How come?"

"Bianca, like my *capruzza*. I gave her that name when I saw her in the Ghost Town. Because she was so white."

"All right," Assunta murmured. "Actually, if the goat hadn't been there, you would have stayed in the car and . . . and . . . ." She couldn't finish the sentence.

"It seems an excellent choice," Francesco agreed cheerfully. He wanted to disperse the puffy gray cloud of melancholy gathering over them. "At least when I think of you, I can think of you with the names you're using."

Santino frowned to hold in his tears. Francesco noticed.

"I promise you that at the trial I'll fight like a lion." He paused, then turned to Santino's mother. "It's hard for us magistrates too, you know? We get to care a lot about a case and then the victims involved disappear . . . ."

Santino started sobbing. "You're the Hunter . . . that's what I decided to call you . . . because . . . because you're going hunting for Pasquale. I . . . I . . . don't want to leave you!"

Francesco's eyes were glistening. Assunta's remained dry. Her pain was still too dark and violent to let out.

But when Nunzia and Uncle Turi arrived, even Assunta gave way to tears. Francesco left the office so the meeting between those who were going and those who were staying could be more private. Santino had forgotten that he didn't want to see Turi. He had forgotten his fear that his uncle would call him a rat. He felt only the grief of parting.

To everyone's surprise, Nunzia declared that she didn't want to leave her Sicily, even though her heartbreak at the separation came out in piercing cries.

"But what will you do alone, Mamma?" Assunta wept.

"I would like to come, but I can't," said the old woman, garbling her words, her arms raised in the air.

"I'm here," Uncle Turi grumbled.

"I'll work in the garden. I'll look after the neighbors' hens." With her moans and without her dentures, it was hard to understand her. Much of what she said had to be guessed. "You know that I would die away from Sicily. I'm too old. I want to be buried next to my husband. You go. You're young, and you have a reason. But come to see me."

"That's not possible, Nonna," Santino broke in, in a tone of authority.

"Listen to him, this *picciriddu*!" said Uncle Turi to no one in particular.

"Eh, what is he saying?"

"We can't," shouted Santino.

"Can't you even come to my funeral, Assunta?" mumbled Santino's grandmother, lowering her arm, which had been raised in a theatrical pose all that time. "If you're not there, who will throw earth on my tomb? How can I die in peace if you don't come?"

In the end Assunta solemnly promised that no matter what, she would return in time to say her last farewell.

PART II

Chapter 22

Ilaria and I are on our way.

We left the harbor three hours ago. When I showed our tickets no one asked any questions. As we boarded the ship, we kept close behind a couple in front of us; they didn't notice that they had two kids glued to their heels. Any strangers would take us for their children.

The ferry was very crowded. We sat down in our reserved seats. "Are we going to Russia?" Ilaria whispered to me.

"Yes, Russia," I answered reluctantly. I'd had it with the Russian spies, but it didn't seem the right moment to tell her the truth.

"What is Russia like?"

"Very beautiful. You'll definitely like it."

Reassured, my sister fell asleep right away. I, on the contrary, have been tossing and turning in my seat for an hour.

I'm thinking about Pasquale. I've been waiting five years for him to be caught, but it hasn't happened: I would have heard it on the TV news because Pasquale Loscataglia is the son of an important Mafia boss. It must have been him on the cell phone. No one, not Uncle Turi, or Nonna, or anyone else knows Mamma's number.

Pasquale used Nonna Nunzia as the bait. Someone must have told him about Mamma's promise. Who that someone is, I think I know. Uncle Turi was there. Uncle Turi, who didn't want me to talk to the cops.

When I called him, Pasquale disguised his voice so I didn't recognize him. Too phlegmy and wheezing to be real. It's easy to do. Even I could manage to gasp for breath like an old man.

It's more and more clear to me how Pasquale found us: from my photo in the *Livorno Courier*, when I won the boat race. *U Taruccatu* must have come across it by chance.

My name was under the photo: Lucio Ventura. A name that couldn't have meant anything to him. But surely he was aware that protected witnesses change their identity. And if he had glimpsed some resemblance—I've changed quite a bit in five years, but maybe less than I think—he must have decided it was worth it to check. It said in the paper that we live in Livorno, so to find out our address all he had to do was ask at the Nautical Club. To get from the address to Mamma's cell number must have been a piece of cake for him. At that point he could use any trick to draw us into the trap. He used Nonna Nunzia.

*   *   *

I flail around on the ferry seat, in a rage at myself for allowing that photo to be taken. Photos on the Internet circulate like wildfire. I have to think this over. It's so hot in here . . . . I'll go up on deck.

I can't be away too long, though; if she wakes up and doesn't find me she'll start crying and attract attention. But Ilaria is snoring lightly, a sign that she won't wake up even if the boat sinks. So I'll just get a breath of air, then come right back down.

There's not much light on deck. I lean against the railing. The pitch-black sea surrounds the boat. I look up and see the stars. So many! They seem to swoop down to suck me back up into the sky with them. For a moment I forget everything. Just like in my boat, when I reach the depths of the wave.

I'm breathing hard. Then harder. The air is saturated with salt, with wind, with stars. It makes me so wide awake. This will be my world in the future, I decide. If I have a future. One last deep breath and I go back down.

Even though she's not snoring anymore, Ilaria hasn't moved; she's sleeping with her mouth open, in the same position as before. She seems far away, defenseless. A small creature in the universe, unsuspecting of her own destiny.

I sit down cautiously by her side, still wide awake: the stars and the fresh air took away all my sleepiness. But I don't want to think about what awaits us in Palermo. What I want instead is to let myself slip into memories, to go back to who I was before I became Lucio.

I was a boy who loved to run. I was the best. Papa was so proud of me. What a strange man my papa was. Shy, anxious. He could spend hours watching a procession of ants and I would crouch down next to him. When he noticed one that was carrying a big crumb of bread or an enormous piece of a leaf, he would be amazed and say, "You see that? So little . . . . Look how he carries twice his weight on his back. What am I saying? Three times, no, at least twenty times his weight. What makes them so strong?" He couldn't get over it.

One day, in the car, he confided that his friends teased him, calling him *u Scienziatu** because he could be entranced for hours at the wonders of nature. A cloud. A tree. A flock of birds. He told me his curiosity began when he was a *picciriddu* and tended the goats.

I remember him as very thin, short: a big imagination inside a modest frame. Even though we were so poor, he kept us cheerful. He did illegal things, like steal. The day I turned five years old, he carried off a silver statuette from a house in Mondello. I came to realize gradually, years later,

---

* *u Scienziatu*: the scientist.

that he stole it. I saw it in our house wrapped in a shirt, and then *poof*, the statuette wasn't there anymore. Papa convinced me that I dreamed it up.

I miss him, Papa. I miss his riddles, the riddles Mamma wracked her brains over. In the end he always had to explain them to her; only then did she burst out laughing. Mamma was so beautiful when she laughed.

There was one that even I had to wrack my brains over. I still remember it: *Cu lu fa lu vinni, cu l'accatta 'un l'usa, cu lu usa 'un lu vidi.*

I whisper it to myself now:

The one who makes it sells it,
The one who buys it doesn't use it,
The one who uses it doesn't see it.

The answer was a *tabbutu*, a coffin.

Poor Papa, he had used it without ever seeing it. But if I keep thinking about Papa my heart will start to ache. I don't want to relive the memories of the Ghost Town either. Not even the hospital—all wretched days to leave behind.

I want to start with my first flight. The first and only, not counting the trip in the helicopter when I was unconscious.

I close my eyes and see myself with Mamma in front of a small white airplane. On the silvery fuselage it says REPUBLIC OF ITALY. Someone I can't remember helps us board and take our seats. The plane circles around the runway, takes a running start, and lifts off. Up, up, and with

185

a few jolts it's heading toward the mainland. Green hills and blue sea beneath us. I'm slightly nauseated.

"That's the Strait of Messina," Mamma explains. "See, I kept my promise that we'd fly in a plane, you and me together?"

"Yes." I'm excited, it's hard to stay in my seat. I'm happy in spite of the nausea.

We were leaving Sicily. Out the window I could see smoke from the Stromboli volcano. Then we were over the ocean, and after a while Mamma pointed out an island. She thought it was part of Sicily, but the man from the witness protection program who was with us said it was the Isle of Elba. Later he told us we were about to land in Livorno.

A car came to get us at the airport and took us into the city, to the place that would be our new home. The apartment wasn't too big, but it was all ours.

When we were first getting settled in Livorno there was so much to do and to discover that I didn't have time to feel sad. I had a lot of responsibilities. Two weeks after we arrived, Mamma found that she was pregnant. She told me about it in a whisper, almost embarrassed. She didn't know before we left Palermo. She thought it was her great grief that made her stop menstruating.

I didn't know what the word "menstruating" meant, so I asked her. She stared as if she had just that minute realized whom she was talking to. She said, "It's women's business," leaving me mystified.

I remember I told the therapist I went to twice a week that Mamma wasn't happy about expecting a baby. The therapist knew all about us; she said not to worry about this. She worked in the witness protection program and knew my story—she was there to help me deal with the trauma.

I vaguely remember confessing to her that I felt guilty over what happened in the ambush. I shouldn't have gotten out of the car; I should have stayed with Papa and Nonno. With me in the car the Mafiosi wouldn't have fired.

The therapist shook her head and said that the Mafia had changed from the time when they didn't kill women and children. They simply would have taken better aim and I'd be dead too.

"That's what I want! To die!" I remember screaming.

We told the neighbors and teachers that Papa had left for Venezuela for work and we'd moved here because a relative of Mamma's had died and left us the apartment in Livorno, with a very low fixed rent. It was the people in the witness protection program who suggested this explanation. We never paid any rent and still don't.

Months passed. At school I didn't talk to anyone, but after a while I began to make a few friends. Mamma's stomach swelled up. She was really thin, but that belly was a balloon. One day, two months before she was due, she didn't feel well. She said her water had broken and that I had to repeat those words on the phone to the Witness

Protection people. They came in a taxi to take her to the hospital and Ilaria was born two hours later. I stayed at home with a pretty young woman sent by the court. I liked her and she liked me. She even explained to me the mystery of the water that broke.

Mamma always said that the taste for pretty women was in my blood.

I went to see my new little sister inside the incubator and discovered that she was a tiny red wrinkled monstrosity. She was hardly human; she ought to be kept in a glass cage.

They came home after three weeks and the lady from the court went away. From that moment on, I became the head of the family: I was the one who had to go out on errands. I helped Mamma all the time. She called me her "little man." She stayed home to nurse Illucia and change her diapers, which took hours and hours. She had no time for anything else. Later on, she started taking her out in a carriage. At that point I could have gone back to being a kid, but instead I continued as a grown-up because I liked it.

Mamma found work she could do at home. We didn't have much money, and the government didn't raise our subsidy. She embroidered sheets, pillowcases, and nightgowns for an upscale lingerie company.

When I was eight years old, she let me go to the Nautical Club and start training for the Optimist races. I had never forgotten that other Lucio I saw at Mondello. Since I shared his name, I felt like I had also absorbed his identity. Along with his talent and passion for sailing.

I don't remember when it was that Mamma, who'd always been thin, started to eat so much. More and more. At night I heard her get up and open the fridge. She gained weight. At the beginning I paid no attention, but then her legs began to swell up and she preferred to stay home. Little by little she stopped going out altogether. She had me take care of Ilaria. Now I did everything.

That was it, until yesterday. How did she manage, yesterday, to go out with her swollen legs?

The vision of Mamma being seized under the arms and dragged out of the house makes me sick. I turn toward the small window encrusted with salt.

Outside, dawn is breaking over the pale, flat sea. There's still a ways to go before we reach Palermo.

Nineteen hours: we left at midnight and we'll arrive at seven in the evening. I collapse on the seat to try to sleep, but I can't. It's no use telling the beastly thoughts that harass me, *Cut it out, you wild little animals.* They go wherever they want.

At Palermo we'll have to get to the courthouse. Will I find Francesco at that hour? I remember he liked to stay late in his office. But would he today? And what if he'd moved? In five years that could happen. What if he was . . . dead? No, I would have seen that on the TV news.

189

Should I have telephoned? No, no. Even if we were friends, Francesco was a magistrate; he would have told the Livorno police to keep us there. Better to surprise him.

He'll say: "Santino, what are you doing here?"

And I'll answer: "Not Santino. Lucio, remember?"

Chapter 23

A little before sunset the ferry docks at the quay in Palermo. Ilaria and I wait for a long time along with the crowd of strangers, all gathering suitcases, bags, backpacks. We're the only ones without any baggage. We wait a good while, crowded on the stairs leading down to the exit. No one pays any attention to us. Ilaria staggers around, leaning on me. She hasn't eaten anything during the trip, only drunk a latte. I had to take her to the bathroom twice to vomit. Her face is as crumpled as her pink dress.

We're waiting for all the trucks and cars to leave from the gaping mouth of the ferry. Finally it's our turn and the line begins to move. Shaky on our numb legs, we go down the stairs together with the other passengers without cars. We cross the belly of the boat where the vehicles were crammed. There's a strong stink of gasoline down there.

Outside at last!

Ilaria looks around, frightened. "Where are the bad soldiers?" she asks.

"The Russian spies? You won't see them walking around on the streets. Don't worry. The Russian people are good."

It's eight in the evening, but the light is still strong and it's warmer than in Livorno. There are cranes everywhere. The port is surrounded by mountains. I had forgotten how beautiful Palermo is. I'd never seen it like this, from the sea.

I'm worried: if we don't find Francesco, if over these years he's been transferred to another city, I don't have a backup plan. The only salvation is my cell phone, which I turned off when we were in the shed, to save the battery. For five years I've kept his office phone number in the courthouse embedded in my memory. He gave it to me before I left, in case I remembered some detail. Something that might help him in the search for the fugitive. Only in that case could I call him. But I didn't remember anything more about Pasquale *u Taruccatu*, only that he killed my father and shot me. So I'd never used that number. All I had ever done over the years was write him short letters that I sent in my own way. I'm not so stupid that I don't realize I was doing it just for myself, as if the great sea I entrusted them to were a messenger of dreams. But now things were different: I was about to meet him in reality.

I hope the Hunter's number hasn't changed after all these years.

I'd like to walk, to save what money I still have, but it's late: I don't want to find that Francesco has already left his office. I don't have his address. Besides, Ilaria's legs can hardly carry her any more. At the information office I get a map of Palermo and find a taxi.

"To the courthouse!" I order, in the manner of someone who goes there every day.

The driver turns around and looks at us curiously. He asks something in snappy Sicilian, something like, "What's the point of going there? Especially today. What do you want to do there?"

Ilaria asks me, "Is he speaking Russian?"

"Of course," I say. Then I turn to the driver. "Make it quick, please. Our father is expecting us. He's a judge."

It can't hurt to exaggerate a bit. Sicilians are always wary when talking to a cop's relatives. In fact the driver, irritated, starts the car and gets going without uttering another word.

The traffic is insane.

"Can't you go any faster?" I ask impatiently, like the son of a judge. It was a mistake to take a taxi; we would have done better on foot.

"The festival of Santa Rosalia is about to begin, don't you know?" grumbles the driver. "We're lucky to be moving at all."

"He speaks Italian too," Ilaria notes.

The festival of Santa Rosalia. I hadn't thought of that. Today is July 14th. Palermo's big holiday. Oh Lord, what if the court is on vacation?

I'm so anxious, I look out the window without focusing on what I see.

There are bottlenecks everywhere, and the man at the wheel seems to be enjoying it. He looks at us in the rearview mirror and shrugs his shoulders with a smirk as if to say he can't do a thing about it.

I could kill him.

We're at Porta Maqueda. I recognize it. I once came here with Papa. I follow the route on the map. We pass the Teatro Massimo. We're getting closer, I think. We go down a street with shops. We must be there.

And there are the great buildings of the courthouse. I get out and help Ilaria out of the taxi. She seems drunk. It's incredibly hot, maybe 105 degrees. I pay the fare—I know he's charged me more than he should, but I don't say anything.

The taxi drives away and we walk around the main building to get to the doorway that I crossed five years ago, sandwiched between Mamma and Francesco. I remember it all: from there we went to the office of the judge handling the preliminary investigations. Before that was the chamber for the lineup. Francesco's office is separated from that room by a very long corridor.

My heart skips a beat as I recognize the monument with bronze wings that represents Justice. Through all these years, while I was growing up, it's always been there, in that precise spot. It gives me a kind of faith: if nothing has changed here, I'll find Francesco in his usual place.

Without realizing it I squeeze Ilaria's hand. She's watching a small group of kids playing soccer in the courtyard.

"Are we there?" she asks in a thin, weary voice.

"Yes, we're here."

We get to the entrance. My heart is pounding so hard it's in my throat.

The great door with JUSTICE written above it is closed. Closed to us. Closed to everyone.

I stare at the barred door with a sense of defeat. Two officers come over. "Are you looking for something?" one of the two asks politely.

I shake my head. Ilaria stares at him with fear. "No," I answer. "I just got tired of playing with them." I point to the kids with the soccer ball. "But now we'll go back."

The officers watch us as we move off toward the group. We stand at the edges of the game for a moment as if we're interested. Anxiety churns my stomach. After a few minutes, when the officers are heading in the other direction, I take Ilaria away. "Were they spies?" she whispers.

"Oh, come on! Give me a break."

When we're a little farther from the courthouse, I stop. "Take it easy, now I'll call the Hunter."

"He's not Russian?" Ilaria asks in alarm.

"No, he's Italian like us."

"I like the palm trees," she says. "They're beautiful."

How about that little goose! She's thinking about the palm trees. Russia with palm trees. When will I tell her that Russia is a fairy tale?

I take out my cell, turn it on, and dial the number stored in my memory under Hunter.

Four rings, then his voice. It's a message. It says he'll be back tomorrow morning at eight.

I blink away the tears stinging my eyes. I mustn't frighten Ilaria. I turn off the phone and stick it in my pocket, pretending indifference.

"Okay, fine," I say. "He's not in now. Let's go look for a café that has a phone."

"Doesn't your cell phone work?" she asks.

"Sure it works. What we need is a phone book."

Ilaria doesn't ask any more questions. She who's always so curious and full of chatter has gone mute as a cloistered nun.

"And we'll get cannoli. Have you ever had cannoli?" I say to cheer her up.

She shakes her head.

"The ones here are totally de-li-cious." Ilaria loves the word "delicious." "The best in the world."

While I'm talking, I try to remember Francesco's last name. Caruso, I think. Or Carusi? Tarusi? Taruso? I'll look in the phone book.

We find a café. Before we go in I take out the roll of *picciuli* and count it. I could kick myself for taking the taxi.

Inside, I ask how much for two cannoli and two orange-ades. After I pay, I still have ten euros. Then I ask if there's a phone. I leave Ilaria, still mute, nibbling away at the cannoli, and go to the phone in the corner.

Luckily the Palermo phone book is hanging on a cord under the shelf with the phone.

I leaf through the pages and find all the Carusos. Under the F's I don't see any Francesco. But I was almost sure his name was Caruso. Like the great opera singer. I look under Carusi. Then under Taruso and then Tarusi. Nothing. No Francesco. I try Baruso, Varuso, Maruso.

There's a Francesco under Danuso. I jot down the number. I have my doubts but I try it on the café phone, to save the batteries on my cell. It rings into the void. I let it ring a long time, while I stare at the wall. Nothing.

What if it's not his number?

I have no idea where he lives. He never told me.

A hand tugs at my shorts. Ilaria. "Lucio, can I have another cannoli?"

"Take mine."

Nothing more to do. For today, I can't find him. We'll have to wait till eight tomorrow morning. With ten Euros in my pocket and no IDs.

Brooding over this, I slowly drink my orange soda while Ilaria gobbles up the cannoli. She didn't eat anything on the boat, while I did.

It's time to find a safe place to stay. There's no way we can spend the night in this café. "Let's go," I tell her.

I've got to think things over. I walk along, dragging my sister by the hand, and pretend for her sake that I know where I'm going. I do know where I'm going: nowhere.

I'd like to stretch out on the ground and sleep. Ilaria asks me to carry her. I start laughing. A nasty laugh. Chilling. It scares Ilaria and she starts to cry.

This is no good. I crouch down on my heels and say: "Illi, do you want to see the ocean? I know a beautiful place where we can stretch out and be cozy on the beach."

"But where's the Hunter who's going to help us find Mamma?" she says between sobs.

"We'll find him tomorrow."

"TOMORROW!"

"Okay, now." I sigh and turn my phone back on. "I'll make one last try, okay?"

I'm still crouched down in front of Ilaria when the phone starts ringing right in my hand. I'm so surprised I drop it. It keeps ringing. I don't touch it—it could be the old man from yesterday. I'm scared. But what if it's Mamma?

With a big sigh, I grab it to answer. "Hello," I say in a really deep bass, to disguise my voice.

"Hello. Who called me a little while ago?"

It's the Hunter. I recognize his voice without a moment's hesitation.

"Francesco . . . it's me!"

"Lucio?" An instant of silence. "Is this Lucio? Is Ilaria with you?"

"Yes," I reply, dazed. How could he know about Ilaria—she wasn't even born when I was in the hospital.

"Where are you?"

"In Palermo."

"Where in Palermo?"

"We're. . . . " I look around and find the street sign. "On Via Amari."

"Where on Via Amari?"

Now I'm frightened again. What if it isn't the magistrate? How the devil could he recognize me right away? My voice has changed in five years. What if it's a trap? Someone who's faking Francesco's voice in order to capture me? How come he's not amazed that I'm in Palermo? How does he know I have a sister? Too many suspicious details.

With the phone at my ear, I stare at Ilaria as if she could answer my questions. I'm about to hang up. The voice speaks again: "Lucio, your mother is looking for you. The police all over Italy are looking for you. No one dreamed you could be in Palermo. Tell me where you are and I'll come get you."

"How do you know our mother is looking for us?"

"You disappeared. She got in touch with the witness protection office and they let us know."

"But the Mafiosi kidnapped her," I burst out.

"What do you mean, kidnapped? She's at home. She's frantic."

Not kidnapped? I can't believe it. I remember how I can tell for certain if I'm talking to the real Francesco.

"What's the nickname I gave you? The last day we saw each other?" No one else could know that. I only told it to Ilaria.

"Lucio, stop fooling around . . . ."

This time it came out as a shriek. "Tell me!"

"The Hunter, yes. The Hunter. Let's not waste time! I'm Francesco, you called me in my office, Lucio. You need help. Your mother is practically in hysterics."

"We're at the corner of Via Roma."

"Stay there. Don't move. Don't talk to anyone. I'm on my way."

He hangs up. Slowly, I lower my phone. My ear is burning.

"Why are you crying?"

I didn't realize I was crying. "Because everything's okay now. It seems Mamma wasn't kidnapped by the Russians."

"Where is she?"

"At home."

"At our house?"

"Yes."

"But I want her to be here!"

"Ilaria, Mamma is safe! The Russians didn't do anything to her. You should be happy. Come on, let me hear you laugh."

"So why are you crying?"

I shake my head in annoyance. She has glasses that make her look like a panda that knows it's an endangered species. But I don't see any tears.

"Be quiet for a while, goosey? Okay? Just keep your mouth shut."

Chapter 24

Waiting on the street, ignoring the passersby bumping into us, I feel a strange sensation. Besides my immense relief that it's all over—a relief I'm floating in as if I'm drunk—deep down there's something bothering me that I can't name. Like a speck in my eye. I just can't put my finger on it.

"Is Mamma coming to get us?" Ilaria asks. She looks like someone who's been sleeping out in the open for a week, but her bright eyes shine in her exhausted face. Where does she get all that energy?

"No, I told you before. Mamma's at home. In Livorno."

"So who are we waiting for?"

"Shh. Let me think."

My brain must have registered something today. Something that brought me a silent little *click*. But my mind, muddled by worry, had relegated it to a dark corner of my memory. I don't know exactly when it happened. After we left the ship, I think. Was it during our wandering around through Palermo in the taxi and then on foot? Something struck me, but what? At the courthouse? The port? Did someone tell me something I didn't catch? The taxi driver? I try to reconstruct my conversation with him. Nothing.

"How long do we have to wait? I'm so tired!"

"Just a little while longer. Keep still now."

"Yuck!"

"Yuck to you! Cut it out."

The more I struggle to remember, the more that something slips away like an eel. I'm getting warm, but not warm enough. It's like when you have a word on the tip of your tongue but can't get it out. The more I think about it, the less I can get hold of it.

Ilaria sulks, but I'm too busy struggling to remember.

"Lucio, can I sit down? Please."

"If you don't care about dirtying your new dress."

"It's all dirty already."

"Go on then, sit on the sidewalk. You'll look like a beggar. We might even get some money for another cannoli."

"Rats!" She's still standing, undecided.

It's like an itch. I need to scratch it. Maybe I glimpsed someone I know? I don't recall any face in particular. And yet somehow I have a feeling that it's important.

I'm still straining to retrieve the memory when a car stops beside us. I immediately catch sight of the magistrate sitting in the back. He opens the side door, but his somber face stifles my eagerness to hug him.

"Get in."

We obey. In front, beside the driver, is the police escort.

Francesco flashes us a quick glance, then turns away to speak to the driver.

The car starts.

"Are you the Hunter?" asks Ilaria. "You don't look Russian."

"Russian?" The magistrate sends me a questioning glance.

"I know everything," says Ilaria.

"Yes? What do you know?" His voice is gentler.

"That our Papa is a famous scientist and the Russians stole his formula and then they kidnapped Mamma but she managed to escape and she's waiting for us at home because Lucio has the formula."

Another baffled look from Francesco.

I shrug: "My sister likes to invent stories."

We're silent. The car doesn't take us toward the courthouse as I expected, but to a street I don't know. "I can't take you to my office at this hour," Francesco says, opening the door. "Please, get out."

"Where are we?"

"For now we'll go to my house. I have to make some calls. Then we'll see about getting you back to your mother."

There's no elevator.

We walk up to an apartment on the third floor. In the hall, Francesco opens a door and we're in a room that looks like a library.

"Have a seat. Meanwhile, I'll make my calls."

Very quietly we sit down on two chairs. Ilaria is intimidated and glances around, barely turning her head.

Francesco's on the phone. He explains that he's found us, and that for security reasons he didn't call from the car—the police escort only started working recently. Then I hear irritated yeses and nos.

"I'll keep them here till you call back."

He hangs up and stares at us as if we present a problem.

"What's going on now?" I ask, feeling dejected. I expected my reunion with the Hunter to be different.

"It seems that tonight, because of the festival of Santa Rosalia, it's difficult to find a way to get you back home. There are no ferries until Friday. They're trying to find a car. The ministry's planes are all busy and the police have all their forces and equipment out for the festival. We'll wait here. Now we'll call your mother to let her know."

"But . . . how can we do that?" I ask.

"Why not?"

"I took her cell phone. There's no phone at home."

A sigh. "I'm not calling your house. I don't even know what city you live in. I'll call the central office of the Witness Protection Program. They'll notify their colleagues in your city, who'll go and speak to her. They probably have someone with her already."

Two phone calls later he hands me the phone with a slight smile.

"Your mother."

After I say, "Mamma," I hear an outburst of tears.

"I'm fine," I try to say, but she keeps on crying.

"WE'RE FINE!" I shout.

From the other end of the line come great ceaseless sobs.

"Don't mention the city where you live in front of me," Francesco warns.

I signal that I understand, and pass the phone to Ilaria. Maybe she'll do better than me. Ilaria takes it cautiously. She's not used to talking on the phone. She's silent. Francesco leaves the room.

Then Ilaria gets going: "Mamma, mamma, come get us. We're in Russia! No, it's not cold. But I threw up and my pink dress is all dirty. I didn't do it on purpose . . . ."

Ilaria hands me back the phone. "She wants you."

I imagine that by this point Mamma must have calmed down. I speak to her.

This time she listens to me. I ask her what happened. I only understand half of what she says. Now she can't stop talking.

"You shouldn't have done it, Lucio. How could you even think of taking your sister to Palermo without telling anyone?"

"I was scared," I mutter. "I was sure you'd been kidnapped and . . . ."

"Kidnapped? Me? And I thought they'd kidnapped my children!"

"It's because of the text . . . I'll explain better when we're back home."

I hang up and open the door to see where Francesco went. After a moment, he returns with a big bottle of orangeade and two glasses. He unscrews the cap, pours, sits down and watches me with a barely concealed smile. His eyes are shining.

"Can I go to the bathroom?" Ilaria asks.

Francesco takes her into the hall. Then he turns to me. "Can she go by herself okay?"

I nod.

"Now, tell me how come you're here."

"I was scared. I wanted to find you to figure out . . . ."

"Figure out what? Did you think you were a super detective?"

"No, but when we got home and Mamma wasn't there I was so scared for her . . . ."

At last I see light dawning on his face.

I have a lump in my throat. I'm about to start crying. I fight it with all my strength.

His hand is on my arm. "Lucio, you're a brave boy. I can imagine what you must have felt when you didn't find your mother at home. But why didn't you go straight to the Witness Protection office?"

I force back the tears and blurt out: "Because you're the only one I trust! There can even be corrupt people working for the State. You didn't tell me! You never told me." I can feel my voice giving way to an infantile whine.

"I didn't tell you what?"

"That there are judges that can be bought off, that even they can go to prison. Like that one in Milan. I saw it on TV."

"Yes, I remember. When you were in the hospital, a little boy in pain after the trauma you lived through, I thought you needed clarity: the good people on one side, the bad on the other. Otherwise you would have been totally confused."

"You should have told me that."

Francesco lowers his head. "You were too young, Lucio. Children see everything in black and white. Now you can understand." He looks me over from head to toe. "Yes, there can be corrupt judges and magistrates, same as in any work people are involved in. When people don't believe in what they do, they can be tempted by money. Or power. That's true. From street-sweepers to politicians, no matter who they are. There's no class or line of work made up of only honest people. Just as there's no class of only bad ones either."

I nod. "Now do you understand why I'm here?"

He sighs. "You should have had more trust and gone to the people I suggested. But I understand you. I do understand. You were panicked. You felt all alone. I can understand what you did. Maybe . . . who knows? . . . who knows what I would have done in your place, at twelve years old?"

I keep still. He waits, then smiles at me.

"But in the future, Lucio, you need to learn to trust not only me but all the people who are working to protect you. In your city. I'm sure there are lots of capable people in their office." He smiles as if to himself. "Personally, I believe that our department is the most honest and committed, even if others don't think so."

The lump in my throat melts and a flood of tears pours down my cheeks and reaches my lips. In an attempt at dignity I wipe them with the back of my hand. I'm not ashamed. Francesco doesn't take his eyes off me. His sympathetic look makes me feel better.

I clear my throat and wait until I'm able to speak, so I can tell him everything that happened in detail. I'm about to begin when Ilaria returns.

"I made a poop," she announces. "It's the first time since my birthday. A huge heap came out. Do you want to see?"

She turns to me and I blush with embarrassment. I glance at Francesco, who's smiling and looking away.

"No, thanks. Go right back and flush."

"It doesn't smell too bad."

"Go right away and flush, I said!"

Ilaria shrugs, turns, and leaves.

I'm glad to have another moment not to be seen with my face streaked with tears.

Francesco comments affectionately, "Hearing her Mamma on the phone must have unblocked her."

"I guess so."

When she comes back my face is dry. I've already started telling him about the two messages I found on the cell, and the text and that cavernous voice that used my real name.

Then I tell him about my photo in the newspaper last year that I thought accounted for how they found me. I keep going until I get to our escape to the port and the ferry.

Now and then Ilaria interrupts, to add specific points.

"I went by myself to ring Signora Agnese's doorbell."

"My brother was whirling around like a top."

"I didn't want to go into that dark smelly place."

"I threw up. Twice."

Little by little as my story unreels, I'm overwhelmed by a sense of how inappropriate my behavior was. Seeing it from outside makes it clear that I acted out of a childish panic.

"Why wasn't Mamma at home yesterday?" Ilaria asks.

I'm astonished by her rational and practical question. I would have liked to ask that myself.

Francesco looks down at her.

"Your Mamma read the text. She thought her mother must be dying, and she wanted to keep her promise. She explained this to me on the phone. Right after she read the text she tried to call Lucio, but she found that your brother had left his cell at home."

"Lucio always forgets everything," Ilaria interrupted.

"So then she went out, just as she was: she grabbed her purse and struggled to a street where she could find a taxi. She took one to the Aqua-Park, but you weren't there. She asked everyone around, but there was such a crowd yesterday that no one had seen you both leave. She lost time calling another taxi; she hadn't thought of keeping the first one. So she went back home, sure that she'd find you both there, but the house was empty, the radio on just as she'd left it. She looked for her cell phone to call the witness protection program, but she couldn't find it. She couldn't even find Lucio's. She was too impatient to look more closely. So she went out again and rang all the bells in the building until someone opened up and let her use the phone. By that time she was more worried about you two than about her mother. As soon as the authorities were alerted, they got moving. They looked for you in your city, though, not here."

"But who sent the text?" I ask.

Francesco looks at me, barely smiling. "An old retired man sent it from the Palermo Post Office. He has a grown son named Santino. His wife was at death's door and he lost his voice from grief."

"What do you mean, lost his voice?" Ilaria asks.

"He couldn't speak. So he decided to let his son know by text. This Santino, his son, a young man of thirty, lives in Trapani. Unfortunately the old man made a mistake dialing the number and the message ended up on your mother's cell phone. It took some doing for the people from the witness protection program to figure that out. It wasn't Mafiosi, as you see."

"But when I called him yesterday, his voice was back," I conclude. "It was . . . phlegmy."

Francesco smiles. "Maybe it was the shock."

"Why didn't the police call me?" I ask, after thinking it over. "I had both cell phones."

"They said your phone was always turned off or out of range. They tried to work out where you were, but it was impossible. Then suddenly they got through. Did you turn it back on?"

I nodded, yes.

"So that's how it happened. When your phone was on, the cell tower could report where it was. But they couldn't reach you because you'd already turned it off again. So they decided to notify me. When I found out you were in Palermo I went back to my office to see if you might have called me. Obviously that was a good move."

Dammit, it's true! Last night in the shed I turned off both phones to save the batteries. I turned mine back on only to call Francesco. It was that last attempt to call Francesco that saved me. And in those few seconds they tracked me down.

Francesco's landline rings again. He answers and says, "I see. So send over a psychologist, someone who can look after them. I'm on call all night. No, I can't. Yes, in an hour."

He hangs up and turns to us, spreading out his arms. "It looks like you'll have to spend the night here in Palermo. There's no way for us to get you home, and I'm on duty. So I can't be with you."

"Who will take care of us?" Ilaria asks.

211

"Eugenia, a court psychologist. She'll be here to pick you up in an hour. I'm very sorry I can't stay with you, but in a couple of hours I'll have to be at work. Normally I would ask for the night off, but I can't tonight. We're under a lot of pressure."

I feel a bit betrayed. What about my case? How did it end? I don't even know how the trial came out.

As if he were reading my mind, Francesco looks at me. "Pasquale Loscataglia is still on the loose," he begins slowly. "He failed to appear at the trial. He was sentenced to thirty years, but we still haven't managed to find him. The other guy is in the Ucciardone prison."

"I know you haven't found him," I say. "I always watch the TV news."

Francesco looks very down. "I can understand how you feel. You wanted us to catch him, like in a satisfying American film. But Lucio, it's very hard. Loscataglia has Don Ciccio's whole clan at his back. My squad has never stopped looking for him. But so far all the information we've gotten turned out to be wrong. One time we got there too late; he had left the hideout a few hours before . . . ."

"A tip-off?" I ask in a faint voice.

"Could be. They have a network of informers, eyes and ears planted everywhere. These past few years the Mafia crimes have been more and more ruthless. Even the old bosses who've collaborated with the police are astonished at what goes on with the new Mafia. I've been busy with so many homicides; other kids have been killed or wounded. The Mafiosi don't even respect their own codes of honor anymore." He sighs, running a hand over his hair. "I'm not trying to excuse myself, Lucio. I'll find him. I won't let myself rest until I've caught him."

He pauses and looks at Ilaria, sleeping curled up on the chair, maybe dreaming about being in Russia.

"I'm glad you have a sister. She's adorable," he says. "So how are things going with you now?"

"Mamma isn't well, she never leaves the house. I take care of her." I point to Ilaria with my chin. "But I'm a member of a nautical club. I have an Optimist sailboat. I'm really into it. But I can only go during the summer."

"Girlfriends?"

"Mm. One, maybe."

"Cute?"

"Fantastic. And so cool!"

"And school?"

I give a lame smile. "It's okay. But I'm not the head of the class."

"Do you still want to work for the police?"

I look him straight in the eye, aware that I'm about to disappoint him.

"I'm not so sure anymore. Right now I'm totally into the sea. Boats. Ships. I'd like to travel, that's what I really want to do. I'm thinking that in the future I might enroll at the Naval Academy. Whenever I pass the Nav . . . ."

Something flashes across Francesco's eyes.

This flicker stops me mid-word: I grasp my mistake. I get it right away: I say quickly, "What I mean is . . . I happened to pass by the TV one time and they were showing a report on the Academy."

I talked too much! There's just one Naval Academy in Italy—in Livorno. And I said I'd walked past it. He's not stupid: he noticed my fumbling. Now he knows where I live, he who warned me in every possible way never to tell him. I hold my breath and wait for my lungs to explode.

Francesco is calm.

"You're right," he says. "There are some great jobs on the sea. I hope your city . . . " he holds up a hand as if to stop me from speaking, "don't tell me which it is"—the hand goes down . . . "is well connected with the trains to Livorno, where the Naval Academy is. So when you're there you won't have to travel for hours to visit your mother and sister. That is, provided that in six or seven years you still feel the same way."

As quietly as possible I release the breath I was holding in. Maybe he didn't get it. Maybe that flash of light in his eyes was simply because he liked my choice. Maybe, on the other hand, he got it all right, but wanted to act as if he didn't understand a thing.

In any case, he doesn't seem disappointed at the news that I no longer want to be a police officer.

"The sea . . . ," Francesco repeats, with such nostalgia, as if the sea, for him, is far, far away from Palermo. "Me too; when I was a kid I wanted to go to sea. I was dying to be a fisherman. On the high seas . . . . Then, life . . . ." He gives a brief sigh, as if he's worn out by his daily life, by what he does.

I launch into a whole speech about the sea. My sea. I tell him how exciting it is to fly over the waves, and how well I do with my Optimist. I'm really going at it. I talk hurriedly, practically swallowing my words, but I leave out that the sea is where I throw my letters addressed to him. From his eyes I can see he's enjoying this, and it encourages me to keep going.

"It sounds really exhilarating," he finally interrupts. He looks at the clock. "We have a half hour. Are you hungry?"

"I'm dying of hunger."

The Hunter is truly my great friend. He's always been. I realize now that when he first opened the door of the police car and seemed so cold, he was afraid I thought he'd given up on our case. I cling to the idea that now he knows where I live. If he does, he'll never tell anyone. And no one in the world will suspect that he knows. Except me, of course. I'm happy about this secret that unites us.

Chapter 25

I've finished the zucchini omelet that Francesco made me. I devoured a delicious local cheese and drank a Coke. Ilaria is still curled up on the armchair asleep.

Now we're waiting for the psychologist who'll take us somewhere.

"Will I see you again?" I ask Francesco.

"I'll do my best to come say goodbye to you tomorrow morning when you leave. You'll be going by plane. Like five years ago. Do you like that idea?"

"Oh yes, a lot. But I want to ask you something. Why can't we sleep here, even if you're not here?"

"No. I'm sorry, but you can't. I have the feeling that ever since you found out that your mother wasn't kidnapped, you're floating in a blissful and reckless optimism. We're not living in an adventure story. I want you in a safe place, not alone in the house. Have you forgotten that you're running a constant risk?"

He's right. I feel so light-hearted compared to that dreadful moment when I found our apartment in Livorno empty,

216

that my life seems normal, like any other boy's. As if, for all these years, the risk of death for being a rat was only a symptom of my paranoia.

"The Mafia is always there, Lucio. Don't ever forget it."

His tone is emphatic, but in his glance I see a bitter sorrow. For him too, the Mafia is always there.

"Yes," I murmur, a bit downhearted. To change the subject, I ask, "Do you know how Nonna Nunzia is doing?"

"I looked into it. She's alive and well. After you left, the village of Tonduzzo took up a collection to get her the false teeth. They really changed her life, those teeth. Your mother knows about this too."

"Can I see her?"

"I'm sorry I have to say no." An apologetic smile. "She's surrounded by people taking care of her. The village was outraged by what happened to you and your family. People were shocked and embittered. Of course this doesn't change the fact that when they were questioned by the police, not one of them would say a word. They're good people, simple and frightened. But they all obey the laws of *omertà*. Only your uncle worries me."

"Uncle Turi?"

"Right."

"When I was in the hospital, he was the one who told me that if I talked I would be a rat. So yesterday I thought he might be involved in Mamma's kidnapping."

"The kidnapping that never was." Another smile. Then he shakes his head thoughtfully. "However, I don't want him to end up like your father."

"Rubbed out," I murmur.

"Rubbed out, or else . . . . I'm afraid he's in touch with . . . dangerous people."

We look each other in the eye for a long moment. I can see he's afraid Uncle Turi has become or might become a Mafioso.

"It's a good thing you don't live in Sicily anymore," he goes on. "Living far away you're safe from that twisted mindset. The Mafia likes nothing better than to find a desperate or poor young man and make him into one of their followers, obeying their orders. It's easy to get involved in crime out of need, or a desire to feel important, or boredom, like so many of them. At least you're far away."

His phone rings and he goes to answer. A little while later a thin woman comes in. He introduces her: "Eugenia Attardi."

It takes me all of two seconds to recognize her. She's the psychologist who was with Francesco the first time he visited me in the hospital. The one with the honey voice.

She studies us without saying a word, first me, then Ilaria sleeping in the chair. From her blank face I gather that we're one more burden for her. She greets Francesco, then turns to me.

"So here you are," she says in a voice not sweet at all. "We looked for you all over Italy. You're really smart, Santino, you got us into quite a mess with your running away." Then her voice changes; she treats me to an indulgent smile, threatening me with her wagging finger as you do with a child who's pulled off a prank.

"Because of you I'm missing the festival of Santa Rosalia tonight."

She called me Santino; she doesn't know my current name. Good.

Francesco runs his hand over his hair. By now I know that gesture: he does it when he's having a hard time.

"It's just one night," he says. "They'll pick them up early tomorrow. Where's your car, Eugenia?"

"Right outside."

"I'll carry the little girl down."

He picks up Ilaria, who's still sleeping, and we all go downstairs.

When Ilaria and I are in the back seat of the car, the magistrate leans into the open door and whispers to me soberly: "I haven't given up. Don't think that. We'll get him. I'll do all I can to come say goodbye to you at the airport tomorrow."

I have a lump in my throat. The car starts, carrying me away from the one person I want to be with.

*　*　*

Compared to Francesco's apartment, which was bright and cheerful, with paintings and some sculptures, Eugenia's is rather austere. There are none of the decorations you often find in women's homes. No knick-knacks, artificial flowers, or pictures of idyllic scenes. Instead there are books scattered everywhere, even on the floor. Legal texts, psychology books. Eugenia is messy. This makes her slightly more tolerable.

I help her put Ilaria to bed.

"That's how my sister is," I explain. "Once she's asleep, that's it, there's no waking her."

"It's good that she sleeps soundly. You should try to do that too. Have you eaten, Santino?"

"Yes."

"Then go to bed now. It's past eleven."

She sets things up in her study, with a double sofa bed. A huge round ceiling fan slowly stirs the air.

"Don't turn out the light," I tell her from under the sheet as she's about to leave.

She hesitates for a moment; a fairy godmother smile flickers over her thin lips. "Okay. Sweet dreams. Good night. Don't let the bedbugs bite."

She leaves the light on.

What in the world is she thinking? Sweet dreams! Bedbugs! What does she think it means if I want the light on? Doesn't she realize I'm twelve years old?

I'm exhausted but too excited to sleep. What a day! It feels like I've lived a whole year. The terror, the relief. Speaking to Mamma was like a magical reversal of reality, as if deep down I thought she was already dead. And seeing

Francesco again. That flash of light in his eyes. He knows where I live. It's our secret.

The only negative thing is that the Hunter hasn't yet captured his prey.

I get up and wander around the room, looking at the spines of the books. They seem pretty boring. Doesn't this psychologist ever read novels?

Half an hour goes by this way. Eugenia must have gone to bed; I don't hear any noises in the apartment. But from the open window comes a great din of voices, explosions of firecrackers, music. The festival of Santa Rosalia is at its peak. Even as the ferry pulled in, it seemed as though all of Palermo was streaming onto the streets. The traffic was hellish.

I look out the window to see the fireworks, but there are only cracklings and flashes in the dark sky: the blooms of light that open like flowers are hidden by the tall buildings facing the window.

But then there's one that shoots straight up into the sky and bursts open way, way up above the rooftops in a cascade of purple sparks. Fantastic.

The only time I went to the festival with Papa and Mamma I was tiny, maybe two or three years old. They told me later that I hadn't been afraid of the explosions. In fact, I shrieked with delight.

After a while, seeing that there are no more of those high explosions, I turn from the window and go back to bed. Even there I can hear the sharp booms of the firecrackers.

The loudest ones make me flinch. I'll never get over that. I get up again and close the window to muffle the noise.

Stretched out next to Ilaria, I try my best to fall asleep. I'm already enveloped in drowsiness—the images under my eyelids are incoherent, all jumbled up. I see the locked portico of the Palace of Justice, the deck of the ship, my sister's panda-like eyes while we waited on the street, Francesco's somber face when he came to get us in the car. Then the cascade of violet light, that scintillating purple that falls silently from the dark sky . . . .

I'm sliding into sleep.

All of a sudden, I'm awake. Completely wide awake.

With the clarity of hallucination, I see the corner of the bar where I made the phone call. Just as if I were there, I see the opposite wall plastered with notices and ads. I was too focused on the phone to really see them—I just stared absently into space with the receiver at my ear, waiting for someone to answer.

One of the ads was purple: a vibrant purple that managed to get my attention without my even realizing it.

There was one word, written in big capital letters, and something smaller written below it that I didn't pay attention to.

The word I had unconsciously absorbed was: *Sibilla*. The Sybil.* La Sibilla . . . .

---

* Sybil, from ancient Greek mythology: a priestess who could predict the future.

I heard a voice from way back: "She gave me everything I wanted—money, women, everything. She makes them . . . what a powerful *magara*."

What does she make?

And all at once I see, as if it were right before my eyes, that cursed gift. The trinacria of my childhood. A wasp in the middle.

How could I have forgotten it for all these years? I threw it in the toilet, crushed, destroyed.

On the purple leaflet in the bar it said "La Sibilla."

Wasn't Sibilla the name of that witch? Yes, Sibilla was the very sorceress who made the trinacrias with the wasps for Pasquale.

Could she be the same Sibilla from the leaflet opposite the phone? How many Sibillas could there be in Palermo? I leap up in bed, gripped by a wild impatience. I can't resist: I have to check. I have to see that ad. Right away. To be sure it's the same witch.

Take it easy, I tell myself. The name Sibilla alone isn't enough. It might be an ad for a hairdresser. Or a restaurant. Or, who knows, a jewelry store. There's only one way to find out: go back to the bar.

I'm already back in my clothes. I make sure the Indian knife is in my pocket. All I need is my shoes. I pick them up and very quietly open the door of the room. If I were to wake the psychologist now, she'd laugh in my face and wag her finger to bring me back to my senses. I need proof.

But if it's her, this Sibilla I'm looking for, if I find out her address, I can bring Francesco a really important clue. A definite trail leading to Pasquale Loscataglia and his father, the *Scannapopulu.*

It should take an hour at most to check it out.

Chapter 26

I'm in luck: a bunch of keys is hanging from the lock. I open the door very quietly and slide the keys off. I'll use them to get back in. I close the door very gently. Going down the stairs, I realize I forgot my watch in the room. No, I'm not going back. It's more important that I have the map of Palermo and my cell phone.

On the street the racket hits me like a hurricane: drumrolls, music, horns honking, songs, firecrackers, excited shouts.

There's an incredible crowd. Groups of musicians, trays of peanuts and pumpkin seeds, cars garlanded with strings of colored lights. Santa Rosalia, the saint of miracles, has brought out the whole city.

The bar where I looked at the phone book is in the neighborhood around the cathedral. I follow the flow of the crowd, since everyone is moving toward it—that's where the procession started.

It's impossible to move fast. I bump into people, squeeze

between them, shove between their legs, and pay no attention to their scoldings.

A thunderous voice fills the street: "You who have brought life with your death. Grant us the strength . . . ."

I study the map to get my bearings. Step by step, I move toward my goal, trying not to get distracted by the smells of sweets, of spices, of frying, or by the elaborate light shows.

"Palermo and its children don't deserve such a great punishment . . . ." the voice shouts into the megaphone behind me.

I pass a stand selling votive candles dedicated to Santa Rosalia. On a stage surrounded by whirling pink, green, and yellow sparklers, a troubadour is shouting verses, accompanied by a mandolin and a double bass. The music drowns out the other, doomsday voice.

The crowd has become a living wall. I use my hands to separate people, I use my head as a battering ram. A big fat tough guy grabs me by the arm. I can see in his eyes that he's looking for a fight.

"I lost my parents! They're up ahead!" I shout roughly.

The big guy moves out of the way. In front of him, someone who heard me makes room for me to get by.

Only now it occurs to me that the bar might be closed for the night. I have to get there to find out.

I press forward step by step, my head down to sneak better among people's legs, until I'm in the cathedral square.

Here the crowd is indescribable. There's not an inch of space. I'm pushed on every side, I can't even move.

The flash of cameras held high up flickers among the sea of heads. I stretch my neck and look upward.

What I see leaves me open-mouthed.

Between the facades of the buildings rises a gigantic red boat, its white sail unfurled. I can't see whether it's raised on a platform or hoisted up by hundreds of hands. And there on a treetop, lit by overhead lights as bright as day, is the saint. Celestial and graceful, with her face and one arm raised to the heavens.

I'm dumbstruck. For a moment I forget everything else. I don't know if the ship is going to move in the procession or not. But I can't stay to find out, even if I'd love to see it sway amid the sea of buildings like a ship navigating through a storm.

I force myself to look away from the vision and hunt for a gap in the crowd, however tiny, where I could squeeze through. It's hopeless. I think I'll never get to the side street where the bar is.

Then right in front of me comes an agitated voice: "Make way! Make way. A woman's fainted!"

I slip into the narrow path made by people moving aside to let the man carrying the unconscious woman get past. I walk practically glued to his back.

Finally, I see the sign for the café and peel away from the man.

The lights are on. It's open!

I go in, again having to elbow my way through. At the counter, people are besieging the clerk with their orders. I head toward the corner where the phone is.

With my heart knocking against my ribs I focus on the wall plastered with notices in front of the phone. In the midst of so many ads, I quickly locate the purple leaflet.

LA SIBILLA
KEEPER OF THE SECRETS OF FIRE
WHAT SHE CAN DO FOR YOU:
Put you in touch with your lost loved ones
Drive away evil spirits
Cure any illness
Overcome the pains of love
Earn impressive sums of money

Vicolo dello Zingaro 33/A, second floor, apt. 4
TEL. 091242455
BY APPOINTMENT ONLY

I'm breathless with excitement. Even if it doesn't say she's a *magara*, it's obvious that's what she is.

I didn't think of bringing paper and pencil, so I memorize the address; then I memorize the phone number.

A sleazy character pushes me away. "I need the phone."

I move aside. I silently repeat the address and phone number. On the way out I stop a woman and ask, "Do you know where Vicolo dello Zingaro is?"

"Just cross Corso Vittorio Emanuele and you're there."

I check the map. It's so close that I'd like to just take a peek at the witch's house before going back. I know it's a reckless idea—I've already been out a long time. But on her front door there might be a sign with a wasp. Or maybe even the whole trinacria. That would be definitive proof. I'd have something concrete to latch onto. The idea is too tempting to give up. It'll only take a few minutes.

As I separate from the crowd, I keep muttering the phone number so as not to forget it. By now I've become an expert at pushing and slipping between people, and I seem to be moving faster.

I find Vicolo dello Zingaro easily. Compared to the other streets it feels strangely tranquil. I slip in and start reading the addresses of the apartment buildings. Number 33 is almost at the end. I stop short at number 29.

There's a car parked in front of 33/A. A white Fiat Punto. In the seat next to the driver's a little kid is poking his head out of the window, eating an ice-cream cone. He looks around three. I don't see anyone else in the car.

What is such a small kid doing sitting alone in a car in the middle of the night?

I'm not sure what to do. From where I'm standing, the white Punto is blocking the door of the house. I'll have to go past it; then I can check for any signs or cards.

I start walking again. The street is so narrow that the car takes up almost all the space. As I pass I brush the hood with my elbow. The boy follows me with his glance.

"*Ciao*," he says when I pass by the window.

We're so close that despite the poor lighting, I can see his little face very well. Cute.

"Is the ice cream good?" I ask, stopping.

The boy takes a satisfied lick of the cone. "Yes."

"Good. *Ciao*."

I'm about to go past the Fiat to finally look at the front door when he speaks to me again. "I'm waiting for the priest." Another lick. "Then we're going away."

"Oh, yes? Where is he?" I lean a hand on the door and bend over to observe him more closely. There's a faint smell of aftershave coming from inside the Fiat Punto. It's a smell that makes me faintly dizzy.

"He went to get his glasses. He forgot them at the lady's. Then he's taking me to eat *babbaluci*.* The best ones in Palermo."

"*Babbaluci*? That's nice. Where?" I ask. Meanwhile I'm trying to peer past the car. But I can't see the front door.

"At Pasquinuccio Dritto's stand. It's the best one in Palermo." Another lick.

"I don't know it. Is it near here?" But what kind of nuttiness is this? I should move on, give a quick look for any signs, and run back to Eugenia's house.

It's that odor of aftershave that's keeping me there.

Another lick. "Are you kidding? It's at the top of the hill."

---

* *Babbaluci*: fried snails.

His Sicilian is babyish. It reminds me of my childhood.
"What's your name?" I ask.

"Toti."

His hair is black and frizzy. He's dressed in a fancy outfit.
A thin gold chain around his neck drops down under the
starched collar of his shirt.

He's a clever one, for sure. Not a whiner. He's sitting
there patiently, all alone at night, waiting for this priest.
I was like that too, at his age. I wasn't afraid of anything.

Could it be his uncle, this priest he's waiting for?

"Where is this Pasquinuccio il Dritto's place? I want
to eat the best snails in Palermo too," I say, to tease him.

"On that hill over there." He sticks his arm out the
window, almost poking me in the nose, and points hap-
hazardly. "I don't know what it's called."

The gold chain gleams right before my eyes.

"Toti, would you show me your chain?"

He slides it out of his shirt: it has a small pendant with
a Madonna engraved on it.

"Really nice," I say, hiding my disappointment. I was
having a fantasy, I was expecting . . . .

"Mamma gave it to me. Look, I also have the one Papa
gave me. I have two of them," he tells me proudly, and
starts to pull a brown cord that I hadn't noticed up from
his collar. "It's a . . . ."

Just then I hear the lock of the house door opening.

The boy heard it too. He lets go of the cord and turns

toward the door, poking his head out the other side of the car.

I go behind the Fiat where I can't be seen. I hear Toti shout: "Papa!"

From the crack in the half-open door, a man's shoe appears, dark and shiny. And the hem of a long black robe.

"Ah, Toti! Have you been a good boy?" His voice comes through clearly in the stillness of the street. It hits me like a slap in the face.

I start running at top speed toward the end of the street. It's only a few yards, I cover them with giant strides and turn the corner, still running. I find myself in a much wider street. No one can see me from around the corner.

That voice returned from the past is still in my ears. It's grabbed hold of my guts and twisted them like I couldn't have imagined them twisted.

The papa-priest. The aftershave. The voice. It's all coming clear: to avoid being discovered, Pasquale Loscataglia disguises himself as a man of God.

This much I've figured out. I'll figure out the rest if I stay alive.

Take it easy, easy. The car was facing the other way. And the street is so narrow that he couldn't make a U-turn. Still, Pasquale could follow me on foot.... His son must certainly have told him about me already. Or maybe he spotted me while I was running away. It wouldn't take much to figure out who I am.

I run run run, a great spinning chaos in my head. How did I ever get myself in such a mess? I'm an idiot. Truly an idiot. And now? What should I do? There's no time to keep blaming myself. I have to stay in the present, think of how to save myself.

There's only one thing I can do. Hide as fast as I can.

There are some people on via Biscottari, but not as many as in front of the cathedral. I keep running for a while, to get as far away as possible. But when I pass a courtyard with a big entrance, I slip in to take refuge behind the heavy double doors. I mustn't be found on the street when Pasquale passes by on foot or in his Fiat. I wait. I take the knife from my pocket and open it. The thin blade gleams in the darkness.

My heart is beating so hard I'm afraid it can be heard even on the street. And after the effort of that run, the scar on my thigh has started throbbing.

Incredible! I tell myself. It's just like in Harry Potter! The nearness of my father's killer has reawakened the pain of the wound!

I'm a little too old to believe in these things. And yet I have no doubts: the child looked like a miniature Pasquale Loscataglia. It's his son. The same frizzy hair, the same fancy outfits, the smell of aftershave inside the car. Waiting right outside La Sibilla's door. And the pendant I didn't get a chance to see . . . I would swear it's the trinacria with the wasp.

Time goes by and I don't hear people running or a car slowing down. A sliver of hope returns. What if Pasquale didn't see me run away? What if Toti didn't say anything to his father? For all I know, he might have been warned not to talk to strangers, and he'd be afraid his father would smack him for disobeying.

If that's so, it means they're not following me. It means I have in my hands a precious piece of information. I know where I'm headed!

I have to let Francesco know. Right now! I carefully take my cell phone out of my pocket, and just at that moment I hear a car speeding by, the tires screeching. I don't know if it's the white Punto, because instead of going to look, I hunker down in a ball in the shadow of the door.

I wait. The roar of the motor fades in the distance. I realize I should be afraid of cars that go slowly, not fast: when you're hunting for someone on the street you don't speed.

Little by little I calm down. I convince myself that the kid didn't say anything. They must have gone up the hill as planned. How long would it take them to eat snails?

I have to call. I peek in the shadows behind me: no one in the courtyard. I close the knife and crouch down in a corner far from the street, amid a heap of old bicycles and baby strollers. I enter Francesco's number.

It rings, then the message clicks on. I hang up. He's on duty, but who knows where he could be? Not in his office in the courthouse. Maybe Eugenia could track him down. But

I don't have her number. I've got to find an open café and look in the phone book. I remember her last name: Attardi. And I know her street. With the confusion of the crowds, it could be a mistake to wait till I'm back at her house. If Pasquale and his son have left the *babbaluci* stand by then, my information would be useless. That's all assuming that Francesco would know which hill has the best *babbaluci* stand in Palermo.

The surge of adrenaline that kept me going at the most dangerous moment is used up, and I'm so tired I'd like to stretch out in this courtyard between the bicycles and sleep. But I've got to get a move on. Now!

I force myself to get up. Back at the double doors, I look out. No white Fiat. I walk at a normal pace along the still-crowded street, one hand in my pocket, gripping the knife.

Taking a different street, I go back to the first café. It's still open. Someone's on the phone. I go closer. I mumble an apology and take the phone book. I move off from the man who's talking and hurriedly look up Eugenia Attardi. Here she is! I put the number into my cell. She answers on the third ring.

"Who is it?" a sleepy voice asks.

"It's . . . . It's Santino." I was about to say Lucio.

"Santino??? But . . . why did you call and not knock on my door?" Then suddenly her tone changes, she catches on. Eugenia's alarmed.

"Where are you?"

"There's no time to explain," I say in haste. "I know where Pasquale Loscataglia and his son are probably headed right now!"

"But what . . . ."

"I'm almost sure!" I'm trying to talk in a whisper, but clearly. "Listen. Do you know a *babbaluci* stand at the top of a hill? The best one in Palermo? They're on their way there. He's dressed as a priest."

"A priest?"

"Yes, a priest, with a black habit."

"How . . . I can't hear you."

I interrupt her, almost shouting. "You have to notify Francesco. Right away!"

"But where are you?"

Again I'm whispering: "Don't worry, I'm coming back now, but you must telephone, please, please! He'll find them there. On the hill. But hurry! The kid is about three years old. They're going to Pasquinuccio il Dritto's stand."

Thank goodness the name of the proprietor came back to me, because when Eugenia hears Pasquinuccio il Dritto, her voice changes again.

"I know that place!" she cries. "But you come back, Santino. Come home right away! Oh God, how did you ever get out . . . . I'll come get you!"

"You can't. I locked you in. Call him right away. Please!"

I turn off the phone so as not to hear her scolding or give her a way to call back. With a sigh of relief I replace the phone book. Now the whole affair is in Francesco's hands. I can return to Eugenia's house. I'm dying to get there.

Unless my theory is mistaken and Pasquale, instead of being at the stand on the mountain, is hunting me down on the city streets.

Chapter 27

I walk through the crowd like a hunted person. It's strange: now that I've carried out my plan and I'm going back to Eugenia's, I'm more afraid than before. How come?

Maybe because up to now I've thought only of practical things: find La Sibilla's house, run away, look for Eugenia's phone number. All these things distracted me.

Yet now . . . it's as if the past has reconnected with the present, forming one united whole: my life. The man who killed my father is no longer part of my childhood memories. Pasquale Loscataglia is right here in Palermo. He's on the run, but he has time to have children. He has the nerve to go around the city dressed as a priest. He takes his kid to eat *babbaluci* while the cops have been searching for him for years.

The foolishness of this nighttime outing spills over me like a bucket of filthy water. Toti probably told him about our encounter. And if he did, I'm in grave danger. Pasquale might appear from anywhere. At any minute.

The Indian knife in my pocket seems like a toy. It's ridiculous. Who do I think I could hurt with that blade? Here in Palermo there are real pistols, and they shoot.

Everything around me feels hostile: the dark, the smell of gunpowder from the fireworks, the white stuff covering the street. Yes, the street is layered with a thick coating of wax from the enormous candles of the procession. It's soft and sinks under my shoes. It hinders my running.

And besides that, there's the infernal din. Firecrackers, drums, horns, cymbals, shouts, choruses of kids.

I'm so tired of chaos.

I see the faces of Mafiosi everywhere, glancing at me suspiciously. Every time a car passes I look for shelter in an entryway, behind cartons and rubbish, or behind parked cars. I've got to calm down or I'll attract attention.

In my mad rush to find hiding places, I've lost my way. I consult the map; I don't know where I am. I keep going at random and reach a huge square where there are fewer people. Here the racket has subsided. It's the Piazza della Kalsa,* it says. The facades of several houses around it are devastated, as after a bombardment. Many of them seem uninhabited. There's none of that sticky wax on the sidewalks.

I study the map again: if I'm at Piazza della Kalsa, it means that instead of getting closer to the psychologist's house, I've gone farther away.

---

* Piazza della Kalsa: a picturesque historical neighborhood in Palermo, now run-down but popular with visitors.

There are plenty of hiding places here, but something keeps me from going up the stairs that lead to the dark and dirty hallways. Addicts could be hiding there with their needles and syringes.

In the center of the piazza there's a kiosk, a yellow newsstand that gleams as if it were gilded. It must be ancient—it has lacy fretwork with ornaments and columns. The roof is pointy and there's a rooster weather vane on top. Around the newsstand are potted plants. I don't know what purpose they serve. They look incongruous in the midst of so much ruin.

I go closer. There's a grating made of little spears. The grating has hinges, so it can be raised. I walk around it. There's a similar grating on every side, except in back, where I find the entrance. I try the door but it's locked.

If I could hole up in there it would be perfect: I could watch the whole piazza without being seen.

I'm the only person near the newsstand. I station myself on the side with the flowerpots: it's the most protected from passersby. I use all my strength to pull on the grate, and it gives a little. Holding it up, I give a quick glance around and jump up on one of the flowerpots. I push the grating higher and poke my head in. I get the upper half of my body in and let go of the grating. With a somersault I'm inside. All in three seconds.

The dark is a relief, but a moment later I realize that once again my choice is not too smart, because the newsstand

is very conspicuous from outside. What does it look like?
A hideout! If I noticed that, Pasquale Loscataglia will too.

I flatten myself out in the tight space and slide down
to the floor. I sit there on the ground, feeling miserable.

I should have rushed immediately to the house where
Ilaria is sleeping peacefully. How I envy her sleep! If only
I could fall asleep too. But horrible thoughts are taking
over my mind like an invading army.

If Pasquale feels threatened, he won't give up the hunt.
He might have told other Mafiosi already. In the end they'll
smoke me out before I can get to the house. For sure,
he's got a pistol in the pocket of his robe. He's capable
of shooting me right in front of his son. He won't even
have to come into the kiosk; he'll shoot me through the
grating. Then he'll put away his gun and go eat *babbaluci*
with Toti.

What am I doing here? When I catapulted myself in
here my shoulder hit the pavement. Now it's throbbing.
I've got to move but it's like I'm paralyzed.

The old scars are hurting. I carry them on me always, day
and night, the damned things. Even if I'm always careful
not to let anyone see them, I'm aware of them.

I concentrate on the noises from outside so I can find
the right moment to escape from this prison. It seems the
festival will never end. I can hear the racket even from far
away. But it won't be long before the fireworks die down,
the stalls of sweets close, the procession breaks up, and

everyone goes home. In the empty streets there'll be only a layer of wax trampled on by thousands of feet.

And I'll be more exposed, more threatened, more in danger than I am now, because in a way the crowd protects me.

Enough. I've got to move. I've got to get out of this trap.

I try to pull myself up but I can't. My muscles won't respond, they have no more strength, and I'm about to burst into tears. One more minute, I tell myself, then I'll go.

Finally I manage to get up. I'm about to lift the grate when I hear the roar of a motor nearing the piazza.

I drop back down and get out the knife and open it.

The pavement is an echo chamber for the beating of my heart. Every beat is a plea: Go away. Scram. Beat it. Disappear. Get lost. Go, go, go.

I squeeze my fingers on the handle of my weapon. Will I be able to use it? How? I have to aim for the chest, strike first.

I start to tremble. I can't stop. Meanwhile I strain my ears: the car circles the piazza then slows down.

It's him, I'm positive.

He knows what I look like, what I'm wearing. Toti told him. So far he hasn't thought of the kiosk, but he can't miss it—soon he'll turn back. Again the terror attacks me. Shrill whimpers come out of me.

I'm a little boy again, just like in the Ghost Town when I hid at the top of the dangerous staircase and waited for death. The pain of those ancient wounds is back, like after a long sleep. The itchy dust of rubble is in my throat. In my mouth, the sickly sweet taste of my own blood.

I feel like a cracked vase that everything has leaked out of: pride, dignity, courage, heart, guts. The only thing remaining in the vase is terror. A terror that fills me completely. A blinding terror.

I surrender to it.

I can't stop trembling and shivering. I close the knife. As I put it back in my pocket, my hand touches the other thing in there. The cell phone. I take it out. With a shaking finger, I redial the last number I called. I swallow. I don't know if I'll be able to speak low but clearly enough. Do I still have a voice?

She picks up at the first ring.

"Hello!"

"Co . . . come to . . . g-get me."

"Santino, where are you? Where are you hiding?"

"I'm . . . in . . . in the kiosk. Kalsa. The piazza. I'm all alone. I can't take it anymore." I burst out in sobs.

So, she'll hear me cry. I don't care anymore.

"You're in the kiosk in the middle of the piazza?"

"Yes."

"Stay there." Eugenia's voice is calm. "Don't move. I'll send a patrol car to get you right away. I'll tell him to blow the horn: three short beeps then three long, so you'll know it's them. Do you understand?"

"Yes," I answer, dropping with exhaustion.

"Now let's hang up. Let me make the call and then call me back in a minute. I don't know how long it'll take the police with all this traffic. Okay?"

"Okay."

As the phone clicks off I feel a sense of loss. The same voice that I once found so artificially sweet and honeyed has miraculously become the one to bring me back to the world of the living.

I watch the time on the cell phone. I'm alone again. My panic is a little less, but I'm still shaking.

I call her.

Busy.

I wait another minute.

Busy.

I'm starting to panic and can hardly breathe. I try again. Nothing.

A new wave of torment is about to wash me away. I take three deep breaths and let them out. That seems to help. I try the number again.

She picks right up.

"Santino. They're on their way. How do you feel?"

"Not so good," I say feebly.

"Well, I'll tell you something you're going to like. Francesco just phoned me. He sent a squad to the place you mentioned. He himself was too far away. The officers in the squad hid near the stall. When the priest appeared they bombarded him with questions. There was a big

244

commotion; he tried to run, but the police stopped him. Can you hear me? They've got Pasquale Loscataglia and his son!"

I laugh. A shrill, uncontrollable laugh.

"Santino, are you okay?"

"Yes, yes."

"Francesco said the officers are sure it's him, although the priest denies it. Right this minute they're taking him to the interrogation room. Francesco will be waiting there to question him. I'd like to see if he keeps up his sham in front of the magistrate."

I stop laughing.

"You don't have to be afraid anymore, Santino."

"I know."

An immense weariness makes my body go all soft and weak.

"They'll bring you back to the house. Do you know, your sister is still sleeping?"

"Yes."

"You were right, nothing can wake her. She's such a sweet little girl."

"Yes. Could you please stay on the phone till they get here?"

"Of course. I'm there with you. You've been so brave, Santino. Even too brave, I might say . . . but . . . you were truly brave to call me. You did the right thing. It's all because of you that they captured him."

"Hm."

"It's not always easy to ask adults for help, and you did that. Good for you."

Her voice is so warm and kind, like an old friend. Even if I can only answer in monosyllables I want to hear it again.

"Eugenia," I murmur.

"Yes, what?"

"I'm sorry."

"For what?"

"Five years ago, at the hospital. I . . . was rude to you."

"What are you talking about?"

"Don't you remember the way I looked at you?"

"A lifetime has passed since then, and anyway it was my fault. It was the first time I was ever in that kind of situation. As soon as I opened my mouth, my words sounded phony to me, pointless. I'm the one who should apologize."

"I made you miss the festival of Santa Rosalia."

"Yes, I don't know if I can forgive that." She breaks into laughter. "It's the first time in my life that I haven't been able to go. You know that for us in Palermo . . . this festival is . . . ."

I interrupt her with a whisper. "There's a car coming."

I hear the six beeps: three short and three long.

"It's them!" I cry.

"I'll be waiting for you at home."

Under the astonished gaze of the two policemen, I slip through the grate and leap out of the kiosk with the cell phone still at my ear.

Chapter 28

In the car no one says a word. The two officers only turn around from time to time and give me curious looks. They don't know who I am, I can tell by their faces. They think I'm a kid who ran away from home, that's all. There are fewer people on the streets now. The songs are less shrill, the firecrackers not as loud, the fireworks not as bright.

They take me to Eugenia's house, and one of them gets out of the car and goes into the building with me.

"It's the lady's orders," he says as we climb the stairs. "She told me not to let you out of my sight because you're the kind who runs away." He smiles. "When I was a kid a friend and I ran off from Salemi to Palermo just to see the festival of Santa Rosalia. They called the police. Same as with you. I still remember the beatings we got." He looks at me sympathetically. "I hope your father isn't like mine. He used his belt."

I widen my eyes, pretending to be impressed: I want him to think I have a father waiting for me.

At the door I get out the keys. "I took them with me," I mutter, opening the door. "I thought I'd stay out only a short time."

"It's four in the morning!" The officer throws me a look of commiseration. He thinks I'm really in for it.

Eugenia runs to the door. Her face is flushed. The officer greets her and leaves the two of us alone. Ilaria is still sound asleep, unaware of anything.

There's an awkward moment, then we sit down in the small living room: I'm much too excited to go to bed, and Eugenia doesn't tell me that children ought to sleep soundly at night. Not even a word about my locking her in the house.

She makes me a cup of herbal tea and gets out some cookies, moving quietly. She gives me the piping hot tea and sits next to the armchair where I'm curled up in a ball. She has a cup of tea too.

She regards me in a different way. I don't know how to describe it. Admiration? Curiosity? Or simply a searching assessment of who I am?

"Santino, tell me everything."

Her face is serious, without any of that phony veneer that bothered me so much. I sense that her interest isn't just professional. She takes me seriously. She's on my side. She wants to understand.

I begin by telling her about my lapse of memory, how I struggled to remember something important that was eluding me, but I didn't know what it was.

She signals with her hand for me to get on with it.

So I get to the moment when it suddenly came back to me after I admired a purple burst of fireworks. The leaflet of that very same purple that I saw in the bar with "Sibilla" written on it. I connected that to Pasquale Loscataglia, because when I was a little boy, he'd told me about a friend of his called Sibilla who was a great sorceress. I tell Eugenia about my urgent need to check this out. So I left the house on tiptoe, searched for the bar and confirmed it on the wall in front of the phone. I describe how I wanted to come back right away to let her know, but since the *magara* lived so close by . . . . I tell her about Toti, sitting in the car with an ice-cream cone, and how at first I thought he was just some little kid waiting for his uncle, who was a priest.

She follows my every word without ever interrupting. I like seeing her so attentive. She's not waving her hands to hurry me along anymore.

Emboldened now, I explain how the clues mounted up bit by bit. I describe my panic: the door opening, the flash of intuition that the priest was Pasquale Loscataglia in disguise. The little boy's father.

"I only glimpsed the hem of his cassock. I can't imagine Pasquale disguised as a priest."

"I doubt that they had him change before they questioned him," Eugenia snickers. "Just imagine that scene."

At that image, crazy noises spurt out of my mouth like the sound of screeching gulls.

"Francesco will be busy with this all night," Eugenia adds, interrupting my insane laugh. "To begin the questioning, he has to wait at the police station for a public defender to arrive. The law requires that there be a defense attorney present. They're still there. He's not sure he can come say goodbye to you in a few hours. They also have to transfer the accused to the courthouse. This arrest is too important."

"But he promised me!"

"He said he'd come if he could. We'll phone him before we leave the house. I'll see if you can talk to him."

Eugenia notices that I've become dejected. "While I was waiting for you I turned on the TV," she says. "On the program *Planet Earth* they were announcing an extraordinary piece of news. Assuming that it's true, which I rather doubt. Quite a curious item. It seems that in these past few hours, from noon yesterday, no one has died."

I force myself out of my reverie. "In Palermo?"

"On the whole island, all of Sicily. They said that even the critically ill patients in hospitals are still suffering quietly in their beds. They haven't made up their minds to die. No fatal accidents, no murders. No one dead in all of Sicily. And we're five million people."

"Is it a joke?" I ask, curious.

"I imagine so." Eugenia smiles. "To make it believable, they quoted reliable statistics. On average a hundred thirty-one people a day die in Sicily. So a day without any deaths is truly bizarre, practically impossible. But not totally. Do you want to watch? The joke will certainly continue."

"Yes."

Eugenia takes the remote and turns on the TV.

It's the local news. The fact is confirmed. The journalist talks fast, super excited. Already some people are saying that this incredible miracle was the work of Santa Rosalia. It'll be a unique event in the history of Sicily.

I start yawning.

"Santino, try to sleep a little, if you can." Eugenia gets up and kisses me on the cheek.

She leads me to the door of the room where Ilaria is sleeping. I wait for her to tell me not to let the bedbugs bite. But she just says, "I'll leave the light on."

"It doesn't matter, it's almost dawn," I reply.

*   *   *

I'm awakened by Ilaria's tugging at me.

"I had a dream about Mamma," she says.

"Me too!"

It's true, I dreamed about her. She was looking sad, sewing a sheet as big as a piazza. Rows of black ants were parading across the sheet. She was whispering: "It's the tablecloth for the Madonna's altar."

"Do you know that yesterday not a single person in Sicily died?" I tell Ilaria. "For all we know, no one will die today either."

The news leaves her indifferent. And yet she was the one who once said there are days without any deaths. After she saw that cat lying dead as a doornail on the street.

She shakes me again. "Lucio, I'm hungry."

"Eugenia's going to make us breakfast soon."

"Go wake her up."

I look at the watch I'd left behind. Six forty-five. I slept for less than three hours.

"No, it's too early. She'll come when she gets up. Ilaria, remember you said that there might be a day when no one dies?"

"Yes," she answers, distracted. She gets out of bed to go pee, promising not to disturb Eugenia.

I stay stretched out in bed. Poor Mamma. Her Sicilian background keeps her tied to that mix of magic and religion that rules the island. The Madonna isn't enough for her; she needs the intervention of a *magara*, the one she believes cast a spell on her for life: Sibilla. I wonder, if there were a counter-spell, could Mamma believe in it enough to order the cells in her body to be cured? The mind can give secret commands; that way her illness would disappear the same way it came. If a person takes a sugar pill for a headache not knowing it's only sugar, in 90 percent of cases the headache will disappear. I read that somewhere.

I must talk to Francesco about this. I've got to convince him to take me to La Sibilla. Maybe she could be Mamma's sugar pill.

There's a knock on the door: Eugenia.

"Get dressed. It's time."

"You promised to let me talk to Francesco."

"I haven't forgotten. First breakfast, then we'll call. I know he takes a break at eight. At eight thirty the people from the Witness Protection Program are coming to take you to the airport."

Only a half hour to speak to Francesco and convince him to let us postpone the trip.

We drink caffe latte and wolf down slices of toast with marmalade. Ilaria is totally deaf to the television, she chatters away a mile a minute. She doesn't want to leave Russia, where her papa is a prisoner. Mamma ought to come here.

Eugenia tells her to hurry, we have to leave; the trip would be too hard for Mamma.

The phone rings and Eugenia answers. She whispers to me, "Francesco," then shouts into the phone, "Did Alfonso Cannetta's killer confess? Not yet?"

I leap to my feet.

"Let me talk to him!" I practically snatch the phone from her hand. "Francesco, it's me!"

"Hi, Lucio. He admitted that he was Pasquale Loscataglia. He's caving in fast. He must have felt powerless, dressed that way. He had a pistol in the pocket of his cassock, but he didn't have time to take it out. His lawyer, the one the Mafia hired for the trial five years ago, couldn't be reached last night, so he had a court-appointed attorney. This also caught him off guard."

"Francesco, I have to ask you something. Don't say no!"

"I can't promise without knowing what it is."

"Postpone my trip for one day and take me to the *magara*."

"Why on earth?"

I start explaining, getting all agitated. "For my Mamma. She's sure she's under a spell for life ordered by Pasquale Loscataglia. Her legs have been swollen for years and she drags them around like an old woman. She believes in witches. The one who cast the spell is obviously Sibilla. We have to force her to undo the spell."

"Lucio, this isn't a . . . ."

"You owe it to me! I was the one who told you where to find *u Taruccatu* last night!"

There's an instant of silence.

"Why don't you persuade your mother that the *magara* reversed the spell? If she's suggestible . . . ."

"Are you suggesting that I tell a lie?" I snapped. "You of all people? A magistrate?"

Another silence. A deep sigh. "It's against all the rules."

"I know. But it might work."

"Lucio, you're asking the impossible."

"I want to know if it's true that Sibilla cast the spell. If Loscataglia ordered her to do it."

"As far as postponing your trip for a day, I've already arranged that. I still need you here. But taking you to La Sibilla is another matter."

I'm not giving up. Suddenly I'm totally convinced of the *magara*'s power.

"Did you see the amulet?" I ask.

"What amulet? The one that Loscataglia and his son had around their necks?"

"That one. The trinacria with the wasp. Sibilla makes those charms. They're all the same. When I was a little kid, Pasquale gave me one as a gift. At the moment he shot me I had his trinacria around my neck. Later I destroyed it and erased it from my memory. As if it never existed. It made me feel dirty, as if I was infected from wearing it for so long. That's why I never told you about it. Maybe if I'd kept it in mind, you would have captured him five years ago. It's my fault that . . . ."

"Lucio, stop thinking everything is your fault!" he interrupted. "This is what we'll do. Your sister can stay at home with Eugenia today. I've already asked the Witness Protection office to change your flight to tonight. I still need you to identify Pasquale Loscataglia in person. It'll be very helpful at the trial, in case he refuses to admit killing your father and shooting you. As far as Sibilla . . . we'll see. In any case you'll definitely be leaving tonight."

"Thank you."

"Don't thank me. I told you that identifying him behind the one-way window is very important. Aside from that I'm not promising anything."

"Thanks anyway, Francesco."

"I have to go back to the interrogation room. It's better not to give him time to pull himself together. In his present state it should be easy to drag other information out of him. You know something?"

"What?"

"Loscataglia said he disguised himself as a priest for love of his son. Sometimes he has a great longing to see Toti, to take him out to get his mind off things. He sees him only rarely; the boy lives with his mother. He promised to take him to the festival of Santa Rosalia."

I don't know what to say. I can't bring myself to imagine that Pasquale has a heart, that he can love anyone.

"How did Toti react when you arrested his father right in front of him?" I ask uneasily.

"There was a woman agent in the squad who distracted him and moved him away at the moment of the arrest."

"And Toti didn't realize that . . . ."

"He realized what was happening when he saw the false priest in handcuffs. It must have been terrible for such a small boy. Terrible and incomprehensible. They told me he screamed. We don't usually arrest Mafiosi with their children present."

Maybe Toti yelled "Papa, Papa, Papa," the way I did.

"Okay," I say finally. "I'm sorry for him. I liked him. It's not his fault that he has a murderer for a father."

"You're right. No kid deserves a father like that. We only talked a bit, but he struck me as a bright *picciriddu*. I hope he gets over the trauma one way or another. Now I really must go. *Ciao*, Lucio."

"*Ciao*."

I understand that for Francesco, children can just be victims, never guilty.

Chapter 29

I wake up starving. It's two in the afternoon. After the long phone call with Francesco I went back to bed and finally fell into a deep, dreamless sleep.

I find Eugenia in the living room. She's made lunch and Ilaria is eating sausages and mashed potatoes.

The TV is on. The news has changed. The miracle of Santa Rosalia, as they're calling it now, was over precisely at noon. From that moment on, those who were destined to die died. The commentators are saying that now that the miracle is over, it appears that people are dying at the usual rate. Everything is back to normal, just as before. It was a break, as if death had taken a day off.

Eugenia no longer thinks it's a joke. I'm persuaded too that something really happened.

I sit down at the table but I've hardly managed to swallow one bite before the phone rings. Without a word she hands it to me.

"Be ready in half an hour. I'm sending someone to pick you up."

I jump up. "Where do I have to go?"

"We'll go to the lineup room in the courthouse. You were there once—it's the same room. You'll need to identify Pasquale Loscataglia behind the mirror. Assuming he's the one who killed your father. He hasn't yet confessed."

"Yes," I answer faintly. I seem to be going back in time. I try to visualize the face of my father's killer. Francesco says something else, maybe to encourage me, but I'm not listening.

What I see in my mind's eye is an image without contours. Over time, Loscataglia's features have disintegrated like a photograph immersed in water for too long.

I collect myself. "And what about La Sibilla?" I ask. "When are we going there?"

"We're not going to her house, Lucio."

"WHAT?"

"Let me finish. Her house is dangerous; it seems she's the *magara* for many Mafiosi. You made a fantastic discovery, Lucio. This woman could be very useful to us for . . . ."

I'm upset and interrupt him. "So what will we do?"

"Will you let me talk? I'm having her come to my office in the courthouse to investigate something else. She gave a man a potion that he poured into his wife's coffee, and she died. The husband swears he asked her for a love potion. He thought it was harmless. We're not sure it was Sibilla who

259

gave him the poison: the husband might be lying. When I question her I'll mention Pasquale's name. You can be there for the questions about *u Taruccatu.*"

I hold the phone close to my ear, calmer. "In your office?"

"Yes."

"But I need to tell her to undo the spell she cast on my mother!" I protest again. "She can't do it in your office. She'll say she can't. She has to do it in her own place, where she has all her magic stuff."

"We'll make her bring all the things from her cave of magic supplies and say they'll be proof of her activities as a witch. Any more objections?"

"Yes. Supposing she refuses to undo a spell in the courthouse?"

"Don't keep pushing me, Lucio. Just stop it. I can't take you there. That's all there is to it. You have to leave Palermo as quickly as possible; you've already given me a stomach-ache with your nighttime adventures. Don't you see you're running risks? Especially if news gets around that it was thanks to you that Pasquale Loscataglia was arrested. So cut it out now!"

I have to accept that. "When is she coming?"

"Loscataglia will be in the lineup at three. She'll come to my office at four."

He hangs up. He seemed fed up with my insistence.

I sit down to eat again, but I'm not hungry anymore.

Ilaria asks me if Papa is coming back home with us.

"I think that for now he'll have to stay here," I say, peering over at Eugenia.

The psychologist gazes at Ilaria. "You have to ask your mother about your father, Ilaria, not your brother."

I shudder at the thought, but I know she's right. It's Mamma who needs to explain to Ilaria what happened to our father, not me. She'll have to find the courage. But maybe it's still too soon; Ilaria is very young and a motormouth by nature—she might talk about it at preschool. Why in the world did I invent that story about Russian spies? Did I want to make our father a kind of hero? Someone to be proud of? That must have been it.

"You'll do just fine."

I raise my head from the plate where I'm stirring the mashed potatoes. "Do what?"

Eugenia tightens her shoulders and leans across the table toward me. "Live your life. We Sicilians are like a world apart. We adore this island and we don't take good care of it. We'd like to abandon it, but instead we stay. We're a people of contradictions. You're going away now. Forget it if you can. If you can't, remember that all Sicilians aren't all in the Mafia, as so many say. Don't ever accept stereotypes of Sicily. Don't hate it."

I look at her, puzzled. "I don't hate it," I say.

Ilaria is watching us. Oddly enough, she keeps still. Who knows what confusion is going through that silly little head?

*   *   *

The encounter with Pasquale Loscataglia is extremely short. Less traumatic than I feared.

This time, there was no need of a stool to reach the window. I've become a tall enough witness.

When the light in our small room went out, the man who appeared behind the mirror along with the two other guys was no longer wearing a priest's cassock but stiff clothes that made him seem like a modern version of an old Sicilian puppet. I picked him out right away as u Taruccatu.

And yet he struck me as smaller than I remembered, skinnier. He was glancing around with gloomy eyes that seemed to be staring into an abyss. With his mustache gone, his face seemed naked, defenseless. His hair was thinner, his girlish hands were nervously running along his sides. Every now and then the tic contorted his features.

Seeing him so cowardly and helpless, my fear turned into relief, mixed with bitterness. A scared little man, just a little nothing who's peeing in his pants.

I wondered: was my father's life worth so little that it could be cut off by such a nothing?

In my mouth was the acid taste of this insult. I gulped, and in a clear voice I spoke the ritual words. "It's him!"

Chapter 30

I'm waiting in a small empty room. Francesco is in his office questioning Sibilla, whom his agents picked up in Vicolo dello Zingaro. He said he'd call me in at the right moment. First he has to talk to her about the poisonous potion that killed a woman.

There's a print on the wall opposite me. It's the port of Palermo as seen in the nineteenth century. It reminds me of another port—the one in Livorno. I'll be home in a few hours.

There's still a lot of summer left. I'll go back to my usual life. I'll sail in the boat. I'll wait for Monica to return and for Mamma to get well. Of course, I can't be sure about this last point. Will a counter-spell be enough to set off the mysterious process in her mind that would cure her? Or is it only an absurd attempt? There's just one way to find out: test it. But to take it seriously, I have to believe it too. Mamma would know in a second if I were faking it.

How the devil can I make myself believe that the *magara* really has occult powers?

On the other hand, who can assure me that it's not true?

Aside from the *ciarmavermi* at the Livorno market, I've never seen a real *magara*, who—everyone says—is much more powerful than a *ciarmavermi*. I try to imagine what La Sibilla looks like, the confidant of my father's killer, but nothing comes to mind.

The door opens and Francesco signals to me.

I go into the magistrate's office. A corpulent woman dressed in purple stares at me with hostility. Her hair is pitch-black, obviously dyed; she has a fleshy face, made-up dark eyes, and lips the same purple as her dress. I notice immediately the heavy ring on the middle finger of her left hand. It has a large amber orb. Trapped inside it is a wasp.

Francesco motions me to a seat, then turns to the *magara*.

"Let's get back to Pasquale Loscataglia. When did he order you to cast a spell for life on a member of the Cannetta family?"

"I don't do spells for life."

Francesco points to the table. "Right. So then what is all this stuff for?"

Only now do I notice various objects on the desk: candles, sticks of incense, a cat's skull, sacred images, animal horns, crosses, ropes, dead scorpions, seeds, herbs, and other things I don't recognize. A whole arsenal of magic.

"I don't deny that I'm a professional *magara*. But I limit myself to curing bodies and souls. I don't use poisons. Take a look, look at my herbs . . . there are no toxic substances.

I do only white magic . . . . That day without any deaths was my work!"

Francesco raises his eyebrows. "I thought that was the miracle of Santa Rosalia."

"But I helped the saint! I sent her my personal spirits to ask for that favor. My heart breaks every day seeing so many deaths. I just wanted it to stop for twenty-four hours. And that's exactly what happened."

"Ah, good for you. But why just for one day?"

"That I can't tell you."

She has a strange voice, slow and cackling, that gets on my nerves.

"I see, I see . . . . Still, it's a great thing, definitely."

I'm amazed that Francesco is going along with her and not telling her who I am. The nasty look Sibilla gave me when I entered the room gives me the impression that she has figured it out. But I can't be sure.

Francesco is about to ask her another question, but she starts talking again in that irritating voice.

"You don't believe me, I can tell. But I was born with a gift. It's only natural, considering my ancestry."

"What ancestry?"

"Garibaldi himself, right here in Palermo, was given a hair of Santa Rosalia by my great-grandmother, which he kept in the hilt of his sword. Everyone knows this."

"The story of the hair in Garibaldi's sword is just an old wives' tale," Francesco comments without losing patience.

"It's true. Because of this true fact about my great-grandmother, totally true, ever since I was a small child nothing and no one could harm me. I'm untouchable."

She pronounces these words with a subtle tone of threat.

'Really? Should we test that? I'll throw you in prison and your spirits will free you.'

"Ha ha, and from prison I'll send you curses that will make you fall to the ground as if you were struck by lightning. Everyone will say it's a heart attack."

Francesco bursts out laughing. "And wouldn't that be a spell for life?"

The *magara* is furious. "No one can harm me without receiving double harm in return. I'm protected by powerful spirits, I warned you. Spirits who command even Death. They'll hunt you down and bring you under my control!"

She's raving mad, I'm thinking. She's also contradicting herself.

Francesco sits there quite undisturbed. "Let's see . . . could one of these 'spirits' by any chance be called Pasquale Loscataglia?"

The woman purses her lips to show us she doesn't choose to answer.

"Because if that's the case, I have to warn you, my dear Sibilla, that Loscataglia can't protect you anymore. He was arrested last night on the charge of murder."

Under her makeup, the *magara*'s cheeks turn ashen.

"That's not true!"

"This boy can confirm it."

"Yes, it's true," I say in a low voice.

The *magara* keeps quiet. Something has changed in her, in her lined face, in the way she holds her body. Her back, formerly perfectly straight, is slumped. She holds her hands together and twists her ring with two fingers.

"Is he Alfonso Cannetta's son?" she asks flatly, sending me a swift glance.

"Yes. That's him."

She stares down at her hands. It's clear she's thinking of what to say.

"Can I ask her something?" I say to Francesco.

"Of course you can."

I watch the *magara* as she grimly studies the wasp in her ring. I try to hide the disgust it makes me feel.

"Why did you cast the spell on my mother instead of on me?"

She jerks up her head, like a snake ready to strike.

"I never cast spells on children! *U Taruccatu* asked me to do it, but I told him no, that I'd never, never cast a spell for life on a *picciriddu*. So then he said I should do it to a close relative of the kid. He forced me to do it to the mother. He brought me a scarf of hers. If I hadn't obeyed, he would have strangled me."

"So you did carry out the spell," Francesco remarks.

"Yes, but not of my own free will."

"And now . . . ."

267

"Signor magistrate, now it can be lifted, that's obvious. If Loscataglia is in jail, I can reverse the spell because he's not in a position to carry out his threat. I don't want to maintain a spell ordered by a killer. You said you're charging him with homicide? He's in jail? Fine. I'm glad. Now he can't do me any harm. Signor Magistrate, I obeyed him because I had to."

"So now let's proceed right away to undo this spell," Francesco says calmly, pretending not to notice the hypocrisy of her words. Even I could tell that this woman was afraid. She'd just lost a protector.

"What are your mother's symptoms?" Sibilla asks me in a tone of fake concern.

"Her legs," I say. "They've become huge, she can barely walk."

"Anything else?"

"She's always sad."

"Then we'll do it very soon. As soon as I get home . . . ."

"No," Francesco interrupts. "As you can see, I've arranged to have all your magic implements right here on my desk. You have to do the counter-spell now, in full view of this innocent child."

She looks at the table with an annoyed air. "And after I undo the spell for life, what will happen?" she asks, turning back to Francesco.

"Afterward, you can go home and all these things will be returned to you. Of course, if the legs don't get better . . . there may be many other investigations to pursue."

"The one about that pig who's accusing me of giving him poison instead of a love potion?"

"That investigation must continue; we can't do anything about it. There's been a death. But we have other cases that are . . . dubious. We can even put you in prison simply for your profession."

Sibilla straightens her spine. Her eyes are flashing. She seems to puff up.

She spits on the floor and commands us with recovered authority: "Silence as the spirits approach."

She's agreed.

She regards us, first Francesco then me, like one possessed. She's already deep into her role as sorceress. Suddenly she's staring straight ahead, into space.

She starts murmuring a litany. "Samonimo! Traponimo! Caligula! Nero! Lucifer!" And then, "The Word! The Word! The Word!" And more: "*Capu noto, capu enne, capu effi.*"

The words are gibberish. Her face is twisted, her mouth half-open. Bit by bit the flow of bizarre words gets faster; now she's talking in an unknown language of guttural sounds like *Gowi! Gooi!*

Francesco and I don't take our eyes off her.

Her face is like a Greek mask, stiff and motionless. From time to time burping noises come from her mouth. A trail of blood starts dripping from her lips.

"*Homn pota capopr!*" she exclaims. "Those are the spirits who don't want to leave your mother's legs," she yells in

269

her trance, then starts again with her rapid-fire language made of arcane sounds.

Suddenly she moves: she raises an arm and gropes on the desk with her hand, without looking. She picks up a rope: a thin braid of hemp. She brings it to her lap and, still staring into space, begins to make knots in it.

"The evil spirits will be hanged," she says in her medium's voice.

After these words more disgusting burps come from her wrinkled lips.

More knots, as she continues her secret litany. It goes on, getting louder, faster. The constant noise of the invocation grows into a prolonged, piercing shriek. Her fingers stop moving. Her eyeballs roll up—just the whites are showing.

Suddenly the shriek breaks off. Sibilla's head drops to the desk, pale and drenched in sweat. Francesco and I are appalled as we watch in silence.

For a while nothing happens. She remains immobile, her cheek pressed against the top of the desk, her eyes closed, her breathing barely perceptible. Her mouth is stiff in an exhausted frown. The knotted rope dangles from her left hand.

"Is she dead?" I ask in fright.

"I don't think so." Francesco gets up and goes over and gently nudges her shoulder.

Sibilla revives, opens her eyes like someone waking from a very long sleep, raises her head from the desk, straightens up in her chair and hands me the rope, with a fixed stare.

"Give it to your mother," she says breathily. "She has to wear it for two weeks and the evil spirits will leave her legs."

I take the rope and look it over carefully: it looks like any old string, a string full of knots. That's it.

I'm so shaken up by what I've seen that I don't have the strength to utter a word.

"Let's go," Francesco urges me. "I'll go out with you." He turns toward Sibilla. "You wait for me here—I'm not finished with you yet. I have other questions to ask. And I have a proposal," he says calmly. "Afterward, you can go home. Meanwhile, would you like a glass of water?"

Sibilla refuses the water.

The magistrate leads me down the stairs and to the front door of the courthouse. He looks at the clock.

"In five minutes the car from the Witness Protection Program will be here to take you to the airport. First you'll stop to pick up Ilaria. Tonight you'll be able to give your mother a hug." He looks at the rope I'm holding in my hands. "I hope it works, Lucio. You have to tell your Mamma everything that happened, word for word. Tell her exactly how the *magara* looked while she worked the counter-spell. Be as dramatic as you can, so she'll almost feel she was present. You might also tell her that the *magara* took credit for the mysterious day without any deaths. It can't hurt if she believes it."

"But do you believe it?" I exclaim in astonishment.

"There are lots of stories circulating about Death taking a holiday in Sicily . . . . At midnight some people saw the same comet that appeared at the birth of the Baby Jesus. Here in Palermo everyone is convinced that it was Santa Rosalia, except for those who remember Don Vittorio and are sure he did it from the beyond. Every city is claiming its own patron saint as the source of the miracle."

"I'll tell Mamma what a great impression she made." I look at the rope in my hands. "I'll say she's an extremely powerful *magara*."

Francesco gives one of his small smiles.

"You know what I think, Lucio? That if something as incredible as an entire day without any deaths could happen in Sicily, why couldn't it also happen, who knows, maybe even right away, that the Mafia disappears? Not for a day but forever? Our island is an incredible place. Crazy. Unpredictable."

I smile too. "Then I could come back!"

"Right. But don't come to Palermo anymore and surprise me. Not until that day. And till then, don't ever forget that even if Loscataglia is in prison, there are other Mafiosi ready to take their revenge. The part you played in his capture should remain a secret, but that doesn't mean that something won't leak out."

"How could it?" I ask.

"Sibilla, for instance. Even if she agrees to cooperate with the courts, she might double-cross us. But she hasn't agreed yet. Or Toti. He could tell his Mamma that on that night he talked to a certain boy and told him he and his Papa were going to eat *babbaluci*. His mother could pass this on to others . . . ."

"What will become of Toti?"

"It depends. My intuition and experience suggest that Loscataglia will be destroyed by the trial, which he's certain to lose. He doesn't strike me as the type to cope with the hard jail time awaiting him at Ucciardone. Sooner or later he'll let us know he wants to talk, in exchange for the privileges granted to prisoners who cooperate with the courts. In that case little Toti will be in danger because the Mafia pounces in a terrible way on the relatives of those who turn informer. In that case the child would be sent to a secret place with his mother."

"Like me?"

"Like you. A new identity and everything."

I think this over. The son of a murder victim and the son of the one who brutally killed him: two identical destinies.

"But is that fair?" I'm about to ask.

As happened often in the past, Francesco seems to read my mind. He says gently: "Lucio, better a father who's a victim than one who's a killer. Think of when Toti will be old enough to find out."

"That won't be any fun for him," I say bitterly.

Francesco keeps gazing at me. "It doesn't always turn out like that. There are people who keep fighting this with all their strength, remember. And now we know that the almost impossible can happen."

I know he wants to give me more hope than he himself possesses. I get out the Indian knife from my pocket. "Take this," I say, holding it out to him. "You can use it more than I can."

He looks incredulous. He takes it without a word, his eyes locked on mine.

"What other things don't I know about you?" he asks in a hushed tone.

I shrug like a man with thousands of secrets.

"I'm glad you didn't have to use it."

"Me too."

Just then, out of the corner of my eye, I glimpse a car stopping not far from us. A man in a uniform gets out and signals to the magistrate.

"They came early." I look at Francesco, imploring. "They came too early!"

"It's better that way. I'm allergic to goodbyes."

We shake hands firmly, like grown-up men, unsmiling. The look we exchange is intense, bearing all the things left unsaid.

"Go now." He gives me a little push on the shoulder.

I'd like to tell him how I feel I've grown up in these last two days. But it's too late. The man who came to pick me up is getting back in the car. Ilaria's waiting for us.

Without turning back, I move toward the car. I settle down in the back seat and squeeze the rope hard in my hands.

But when the car starts, I can't resist. I look out the back window at the slender figure of the magistrate. He's standing in front of the door, still as a statue. He sticks the Indian knife in his pocket and with a slow gesture raises both his hands to say goodbye to me. His hands are waving excitedly. The goodbye of an exuberant kid.

I'll always remember him that way, with his arms raised in the air, as if they wanted to keep the heavy stone letters of the word JUSTICE from falling on his head.

ABOUT THE AUTHOR

Silvana Gandolfi has written many acclaimed books for young people and is one of Italy's most widely translated authors. Her novel for children *Aldabra, or The Tortoise Who Loved Shakespeare* has also been translated into English by Lynne Sharon Schwartz. Among her numerous awards is the Andersen Prize, Italy's most important prize for children's literature. She lives in Rome.

ABOUT THE TRANSLATOR

Lynne Sharon Schwartz has published twenty-five books of fiction, nonfiction, essays, poetry and translation. Her reviews and criticism have appeared in many leading magazines and newspapers. She has received grants from the Guggenheim Foundation, the National Endowment for the Arts, and the New York State Foundation for the Arts, and has taught in writing programs in the United States and abroad. She is presently on the faculty of the Bennington Writing Seminars.